GIRL ONE:

MURDER

(A Maya Gray FBI Suspense Thriller—Book 1)

Molly Black

Molly Black

Debut author Molly Black is author of the MAYA GRAY MYSTERY series, comprising three books (and counting).

An avid reader and lifelong fan of the mystery and thriller genres, Molly loves to hear from you, so please feel free to visit www.mollyblackauthor.com to learn more and stay in touch.

ISBN: 978-1-0943-9276-9

CHAPTER ONE

Maya Gray of the FBI's Cold Case Unit sat in her rental car, looking over a small house in the suburbs of Harristown, Missouri. It was freshly painted, with an actual white picket fence. The kind of place that developers loved to sell as the real American dream, even if Maya herself had never really dreamed of anything like it. Number thirteen.

She checked a copy of the case file on her phone to make sure that she had the right address, mentally going over the details of the case. Even for a routine visit like this, it was important to Maya that she had her facts straight.

Ok, so Ben Harrow had been found dead in a woodland ten years ago, in a protected area known for its rare flowers. He'd been stabbed repeatedly. A ring had been taken from him, as well as the contents of his wallet, presumably in a clumsy attempt to make it look like a robbery. Maya had all that already, but she read through anyway, making sure that she didn't miss anything.

Today, she was due to talk to Timothy Jameson, a friend of Harrow's. The file said original investigation had talked to him, so Maya needed to go over the same ground, even if it didn't look to Maya like he would have much to tell her.

Taking a breath, she walked up to the house and rang the doorbell.

It took a while before anyone within answered, although the Toyota in the driveway indicated that someone was home. Maya could imagine Mr. Jameson looking at her through a peephole, or maybe with a camera, trying to judge if it was a good idea to answer.

This was where it helped to look like she did. She was tall for a woman, at almost five feet ten inches, and athletic, but the suit she wore hid most of that, making her look more delicate than she was. Her dark hair was tied back as professionally as possible, but a strand or two always got free. Maya didn't bother with makeup, but even at thirty-five, her features had a kind of youthful glow to them that could pass for pretty in the right light. Her mouth tended to naturally quirk into a smile, even when there was no reason for it.

She knew she didn't look threatening, and she found that made it easier to get people to help her. Even so, she wondered if it would be enough to get her in the door today, or if she would be left standing there. One of the benefits of not having a partner was that there would be no one to laugh if the homeowner simply ignored her.

Maya breathed a sigh of relief when a middle-aged man opened the door. He was rugged looking, in that "formerly a quarterback but now living too well" kind of way, taller than her, with unkempt brown hair, dark eyes, and a frame running slightly towards fat. He wore slacks and a t-shirt and looked Maya over far too openly for her taste.

"Timothy Jameson?" Maya asked with her best smile.

"And you are?" he replied.

It didn't feel to Maya like the kind of suspicion of possible cops she got in some places. Maybe he was worried that she was there to try to sell him something.

"Agent Gray, FBI Cold Case unit," she explained.

She took out her ID to show him. He took the time to look it over carefully.

"I was hoping to ask you a few questions about the Ben Harrow case," Maya said. "Just routine."

"You're looking into that now?" Jameson asked, with a note in his voice that might have been irritation, or worry, or both. Maya was no expert, though.

"I'm going back through the files," Maya replied. She didn't want him thinking that this was a full-scale investigation when it wasn't. She didn't want to get his hopes up. "We like to review them every so often. But it would be helpful if you could answer a couple of questions for me. May I come in?"

He hesitated. Maya had found that even the most law-abiding people hesitated when the FBI asked to come in, usually wondering if they'd left anything illegal lying around.

Maya hoped that Jameson would let her in, though. He'd been one of Ben Harrow's closest friends, working with him at the same insurance company for years. Maya found that the more she could learn about a victim's life, the better, and Jameson was one of the best people to tell her more.

"Yeah, I guess that would be ok," Jameson said. "Although I don't know what I can tell you that I haven't already said."

"Sometimes, enough time passing can give people a different perspective on events," Maya said, stepping inside. The house had

2

obviously started off as a neat, well-kept family home, but now it was untidy, with empty pizza boxes resting on the arm of one of the chairs as Jameson led the way through to the living room.

Maya took in the details of the place as she walked in. House plants on just about every surface that would hold them. Furniture worn and leather. There were bookshelves, where the contents seemed to be a random mix of sci-fi, fishing books, and practically a whole case on gardening and plants.

"Take a seat," Jameson said. "Iced tea?"

"Thank you," Maya said. Sitting among the plants sipping iced tea was a long way from her usual round of interview rooms and dusty files.

"How does someone like you end up working in the FBI, anyway? You seem too... nice for it."

"I joined out of the army," Maya said.

He looked at her like he could barely believe it. Maya was used to that. Even her parents had found it strange that their baby girl had gone off to fight, and then joined the FBI. Her mother still asked her when they FaceTimed if she didn't want to find something safer to do.

"I just wanted to talk about the night Ben Harrow disappeared," Maya said, taking the seat he'd gestured towards. "Anything you remember might help. Any small detail."

"I'm not sure how much I do remember," Jameson said. "I mean, I want to help, but going over all of this again is difficult."

"I know," Maya said. She knew better than anyone what it was like when someone close was missing or dead. "But sometimes time can let you remember things you didn't before. And the more you can tell me about Ben, the better. What was he like?"

"He was one of those guys who was always the life and soul of the party," Timothy said. "People liked him. He was an outdoors guy, didn't like being cooped up in an office all day. When he found out that I liked to hike and catalogue wildflowers, he insisted on coming along."

"You and Ben used to go up to the woods where he was found?" Maya asked.

"Hiking," Jameson agreed. "He used to like the chance to be outdoors, and I would go up for the chance to check the rare flowers in the reserve. It... it still feels horrible, imagining him lying there among the Western Prairie Fringed Orchid like that."

"Yes," Maya agreed, although she wasn't sure that she would recognize the flower if she saw it. She'd never been a flowers kind of girl growing up. She *did* recognize the name, though, and something about it nagged at her.

Maya knew better than to try to force the issue. When a thought like that wouldn't come to her, she found it was usually better to leave it until it was ready. Instead, she kept going with the questions she wanted to ask.

"Now, part of the reason I wanted to talk to you was that, at the time, you had some theories about what might have happened to Ben. You talked about him owing money to some dangerous people. Do you have any more details of who those people might be?"

Maya saw Timothy look surprised by the question.

"Oh, that... that's a little embarrassing," he said. "You see, I don't *have* any details. The FBI were asking me all these questions, because... well..."

"Because it came out in the investigation that Ben was sleeping with your wife," Maya said.

"Yes," Jameson said. There was a flash of anger there in his voice.

Maya had found that, working cold cases. Everyone thought the emotions would fade over time, but they didn't. They hadn't in her life, either.

"I know the original inquiry briefly looked at you as a suspect," Maya said. "They thought you had a motive, but you had an alibi. So tell them the rest?"

"I didn't make it up, exactly," Timothy said, sounding defensive. "I had a vague idea that Ben might be in trouble, so I told them. I just don't know any details of it."

Maya tried to make some sense of that. She had to work out just how much truth there had been in all of this.

"Why do you want to come here and stir up the past?" he demanded.

"It's my job," Maya pointed out. "Cold cases, remember?"

"Didn't want to be where the action was?" Jameson asked. There was a sharp edge to that, and Maya suspected that he was trying to get her to react just so that he didn't have to talk about difficult things. She could see him fidgeting in place, playing with a ring that she suspected was his old wedding ring.

Actually, Maya had wanted all the action when she'd joined the FBI. She'd dreamed of charging in on drug raids or taking down terrorist cells. She'd stumbled into the Cold Cases Unit, but then she'd realized that she had the chance to do plenty of good. She could bring

4

closure to families after years of wondering about the truth. She could put away killers long after they thought they'd gotten away with it. It was where she wanted to be.

"It's more fulfilling than you might think," Maya said.

"What? Sorting through things where there's nothing to find out?" Jameson asked. He clearly didn't like her bringing up the affair. His body language had hunched in protectively, so that he looked a little smaller now.

He hesitated for a moment or two. "I'm sorry. When what Ben and Dianne were doing came out in the original investigation, the divorce ended up being rough."

"No, I'm sorry," Maya said. The feeling of something at the back of her mind was still there. "You had an alibi, though."

"I was at a camp site fifty miles away," Jameson agreed. "I like to camp out. Just me, and the stars, and the wilderness."

There was something about that, too, but it was a little easier to put her finger on.

"If you prefer it to be just you, why a camp site? Is that what you would normally do?" Maya asked.

Jameson shrugged. "I felt like a change."

Maya sat there, feeling like something was starting to shift in her mind. Some sense of things being wrong here was starting to wake up in her. It was nothing, probably less than nothing, but to Maya, going camping in front of other people when he normally camped out alone felt like the kind of thing someone might do if they were *trying* to establish an alibi.

Then there was his not quite a lie to the original investigation. Ok, so maybe he was trying to be helpful, and Maya could understand someone wanting to deflect attention from themselves, but again, something about it made Maya want to take a closer look at Timothy Jameson.

She'd come to Timothy Jameson as something just routine, but now, she was starting to have suspicions about him. He was certainly reacting more to her questions, with small movements, like he wanted to dart up out of his seat and be anywhere else but here.

"Can you tell me more about anything you *do* remember from that time?" Maya said. "The more you can tell me, the more chance I have of finding Ben's killer."

"There isn't really anything," Timothy said. "As I think we've established with the fact I missed that my wife was having an affair with my best friend, I wasn't exactly the best at spotting details."

No, Maya supposed that she could understand that. She took out her phone to glance at the file again, wanting to make sure that she hadn't missed anything, but mostly wanting an excuse to think for a moment.

As she stared at the file, Maya remembered where she'd heard about the Western Prairie Fringed Orchid before.

The enormity of it made her palms suddenly sweaty and made her want to blurt out what she thought she knew. No, she had to be more careful than that. She had to check that she hadn't misheard. She watched Jameson and thought that she could see a small bead of sweat forming on his brow.

"I'm sorry," Jameson said. "Is that everything? I have things I need to do."

"Just one thing," Maya said. "You know flowers, right?"

"I would like to think so," Jameson agreed. It even seemed to take away some of the hostility that had come up between them.

"What were the ones Ben was lying among again? I can never get these things straight."

"The Western Prairie Fringed Orchid," Jameson said.

Those words hit Maya like lead weights. She had to fight to keep her reaction off her face, because inside... well, inside, she was freaking out, almost panicking. She stared at Timothy Jameson, trying to fit the pieces together.

In that moment, she was certain that she was in the room with Ben Harrow's killer.

Maya knew what she should do. She should leave like nothing had happened and come back with backup. But what if Jameson realized his mistake the moment she was gone? What if he disappeared while Maya was waiting for backup?

No, she had to do this, right now. There was no other way.

Maya nodded to herself and rose from her seat, trying to make it look as normal as possible, in spite of the sudden mix of fear and adrenaline coursing through her. To Jameson, it probably looked like she was getting ready to leave.

Maybe she could have just drawn her service weapon then and told him to get down on the floor, but she wanted to hear confirmation first. Maybe there was another explanation for this she hadn't thought of.

6

"How do you know that, Timothy?" Maya asked. "How did you know that it was *there*, specifically, and not in some other part of the forest?"

She saw the change in his expression, the sudden realization that he'd said the wrong thing.

"Someone… someone must have told me."

"It was a detail we never released to the public."

That was standard practice: hold some details back, so that they could weed out all the crazies and the attention seekers claiming to have committed a crime. Have something that they could verify. As far as the public weas concerned, the murder had taken place in an ordinary section of forest.

Maya stared at Jameson, and he stared back at her. She saw something in his expression shift, becoming colder and more dangerous. There was a kind of fury there that hadn't been there before, barely contained.

Maya started to reach for her Glock, because in that moment she desperately wanted a gun on him. Jameson was faster, though, charging forward with all the speed and strength of a former football player.

Maya had a fraction of a second to make a decision. She abandoned her attempt to get to her gun, because that was a recipe for wrestling over it and just praying that she didn't get shot with her own weapon. Besides, was she really going to shoot an unarmed man?

Instead, she hit Jameson as he came in with the best punch she could manage, putting all her weight behind it as he came forward. She heard Jameson groan with the connection, but even so, the momentum of his charge was enough to bear them both back into the chair Maya had been sitting on.

The whole thing tipped over to the ground, so that Maya hit with a jarring impact. There, he struggled to come up on top, presumably reasoning that he could beat Maya senseless while she lay there.

Adrenaline cut through the pain of being slammed to the ground, and Maya reacted on instinct. She'd trained for this. She knew how to fight. Even as Timothy tried to rear up, she hooked a leg under his thigh, turning and flipping him over, so that now, she was the one on top.

Even from there, he tried to punch at her, and he was strong enough that when the strikes connected, they hurt; but he was on the bottom now, and he didn't have gravity on his side behind the blows. Maya gritted her teeth and took the ones she had to, staying on top, trapping Jameson's arms as best she could.

He tried to buck her clear, but she rode the movement, letting him turn as he tried to stand so that she ended up behind him. She kept her weight on him, ignoring his flailing, grabbing one of his arms and working to wrench it behind his back. He was strong, strong enough that Maya started to think that she might not be able to do it.

She had to pivot her whole body around to manage it, and the moment she got her cuffs on one wrist, that just meant that Jameson flailed harder with his other arm. It caught her at the side of her head, and for a moment, Maya saw stars.

Maya had put in enough training to react automatically, even then. She grabbed the flailing arm and clung to it, finally managing to get the handcuffs round it. She snapped them into place, ignoring his attempts to thrash clear even now.

Maya dared to breathe a sigh of relief.

She'd just caught a killer who'd eluded justice for ten years. In that moment, Maya felt a kind of satisfaction that only came from bringing a murderer to justice. At the same time, she knew as well as anyone just how thin the evidence still was. One comment that only she'd heard? The fact that Jameson had attacked her? It was a start, but this was case still far from done.

Still, as Mayah rose unsteadily to her feet, holding Jameson, she pictured the convict sitting behind bars who would write her once a month, even after all these years, insisting he wasn't the one who'd killed Harrow, that they had jailed the wrong man. She pictured his children, constantly imploring her to investigate the case and to free their father. She could see even now their tears of joy to finally have their father back.

Behind it, Mayah pictured the dozens of other case files on her desk, all brimming, all demanding her attention.

And she couldn't wait to get back to work in the morning.

CHAPTER TWO

Maya headed into the office as soon as she got off the red-eye. Six AM wasn't the earliest she'd gone into work, by a long shot. She wanted to get through the paperwork on the Harrow case, and then get started on the backlog of other cases sitting on her desk.

There were always more cold cases, always more families in need of closure.

At this hour of the morning, there was only a skeleton crew in the FBI headquarters in Washington, DC, so the lobby was largely empty as she went through the security checks and headed up to the fifth floor.

That should have been even emptier, because this hour of the morning was normally reserved for those parts of the bureau that had time sensitive cases. Maya actually liked being in there alone, in the middle of the vast bullpen of the fifth floor, with no one to distract her.

As she got out of the elevator, though, she saw that she wasn't the only one who'd had that idea. Maybe three other agents were spread out around the bullpen, working on their cases.

"Gray! What are you doing here this early?"

To her, Harris always looked like someone's rich uncle, with a suit Maya was sure she couldn't have afforded, a gold clip holding his tie, and his head shaved to hide the spot where he was balding. His body had a slight softness to it, and his features had a broad openness to them that Maya suspected might make people think he was stupid, but she knew far better than that by now.

"I wanted to get the paperwork done on the Harrow case," Maya said.

"And start another three cases?" Harris guessed. "My office, Gray. Now."

There was a sharpness to that order that got her a look of sympathy from a couple of tired looking agents who glanced up from their work at the sound. Maya felt a little like she was being summoned to the principal's office back at school. That had happened more than a few times. She made her way across the bullpen, to the spot where the door to Harris's office stood open, waiting for her. Would he be angry about the way the Harrow case had turned out?

9

The space within had that feel to Maya of somewhere the occupant didn't intend on moving from anytime soon. She spotted the pictures of Harris' family set out on the desk, and the pictures hung on the wall of Harris with at least three former Presidents. He'd actually put a hat stand in one corner, in what Maya suspected was a deliberate affectation, from which his tactical jacket was hanging.

"Come in, Gray," he said, loud enough that Maya was sure it would carry out to the few agents who were there this early. "Shut the door."

Maya did as she was told and couldn't stop herself from standing at attention in front of Harris's desk, like she was about to be court-martialed.

"I know things didn't exactly work out the way I might have planned in the Harrow case," Maya began, "but-"

"Oh, don't bother with all that," Harris said, in a reassuring tone that seemed completely at odds with the sharpness before. It left Maya wondering precisely what was going on.

"Sir?" Maya said.

"What? You think I'm going to chew you out for catching a murderer?" Harris said, and now he looked amused. "That was just for the benefit of everyone out there, so they don't think you just get away with taking risks."

Maya was so relieved, that she almost laughed. She dared to relax a little, although she couldn't help pointing out the ways that things still weren't simple. She felt almost as if she was playing Harris's part in this conversation now.

"We still only have an admission that wasn't recorded, and a slightly weak alibi," Maya said.

Harris waved that away. "He attacked an agent, too. That will let us hold him and look closer. He'll break. Now we *know* he did it, the evidence will stack up."

Maya wished that she had his easy confidence about these things. There would still be a lot of details to get right with all this, a lot of traces to follow. Still, she had to hope that she could do it.

"I wanted to congratulate you personally," Harris said. Maya caught the knowing look out towards the bullpen. "And yes, make sure that everyone understands how dangerous it was for you to walk in to talk to a suspect alone."

"He wasn't a suspect," Maya pointed out, trying to cut off Harris's objections. "I thought he was just a witness."

"Even so, going in alone was dangerous," Harris said.

10

Maya couldn't really argue with that, not when she'd stumbled straight into a hand-to-hand confrontation with a murderer. She could guess what he was going to say next, mostly because they'd had this conversation before.

"You need a partner," Harris said.

"I don't," Maya replied. "You can't spare the personnel for cold cases, and I can always partner with local PD when I need them."

She didn't *want* a partner. She liked working alone. Every person too close to her was someone who might get hurt. Someone else she had to worry about.

"So you keep saying," Harris said. "But you can't keep going into situations on your own, Gray. You *need* a partner."

"If I'd known it would be a situation, I would have brought backup," Maya replied. She wasn't about to be pushed into having a partner she didn't want or need. "Seriously, I work cold cases. Ninety-nine percent of what I do is routine."

"And the other one percent?" Harris asked.

Maya shrugged. "I deal with. I can take care of myself, sir."

Taking care of herself was the easy part. It was when she had to take care of other people too that things got complicated.

"Take the rest of the day to think about it," Harris said.

"Sir?" Maya said, looking at him in surprise.

Harris's expression was firm. "I'm sending you home, Gray. Not even you can close a case, come straight in off the red-eye, and expect to do a good job. Take the day off. Get some actual rest."

Maya didn't want rest. She wanted to get on with the next case. Every second she took without doing so would feel like ants crawling on her skin, like she was letting down some family out there that could have answers.

"Sir, I'm fine," Maya said. "I still have-"

Harris didn't give any indication of backing down. It was sometimes easy to forget the steel it must have taken to reach his position.

"Take the rest of the day," he said. "Even you need time to recover after going toe-to-toe with a murderer. If you argue, if I see you before 9am tomorrow, I'll make you take the week."

Maya knew when she was beaten. "Yes sir."

*

Maya had heard somewhere that almost nobody actually lived in Washington, DC. Oh, there were plenty of people who passed through, or stayed there for a while to be near the seat of political power in the country, or had jobs that made them need to be there, but no one thought of it as home.

Maya guessed that made her the exception. She traveled all across the country with her work, but wherever she was, DC was ready to call her back. When she unlocked the door to her apartment, it was like gravity had pulled her back into her natural resting spot.

The moment she'd seen the open plan spaciousness of her apartment, Maya had known that it was perfect for her. It was on the third floor of her building, with views out towards the Capitol Building that made Maya think of the whole thing more like a postcard than an actual place.

When it came to furniture. She'd taken the time to set up a small gym area in a corner with a punchbag and a few weights, and if that ate into the living space a little, well, it wasn't like she had people around much. She had more than enough for herself with a couple of chairs and a TV bolted to the wall. The kitchen was small, but since Maya ate takeout or microwaved her dinner as often as cooking, she didn't care much. Her bed sat off in the back corner. Maya had made it with military corners before she left, because she found that some habits die hard.

No one welcomed her home. Maya preferred things that way, or at least, she was pretty sure that she didn't have time for anything right now. There had been a couple of guys in the past, but none of them had lasted. What was it her last boyfriend had said?

"I can't take being in second place to a bunch of dead people."

Something like that, at least. It had hurt, enough that Maya had told him to get out there and then. Probably the worst part was that Maya hadn't been able to argue with the sentiment even a little. Her work, her career, came first, and had done so since she first joined the military. When she'd gone to college, she'd been shocked to see people just drifting through it without the sense of purpose that had made her a straight A student.

Maya ordered in pizza and then sat down to watch TV with cranberry juice out of the refrigerator. She heard a neighbor's dog bark downstairs and, not for the first time, wondered if she should get one of her own. That wouldn't be fair, though, when she was away so much. She was fine just as she was, alone.

Maya sat like that for a while, because she was pretty sure that was what most other people did with their lives. It wasn't what she wanted to do, though. Every moment she spent like this felt like a moment she was wasting. Maybe that was a good reason to hold back, though. Some obsessions weren't healthy.

As much as she tried to tell herself that she ought to just relax for a while, she knew that she couldn't. Instead, Maya went over to the small corner of the apartment that she used as an office, starting up her laptop and opening up the metal filing cabinet she'd bought with a small key.

Maya took out a mix of files. There were a trio of folders by now, all devoted to the same thing: her sister, Megan.

Just the thought of Megan's name made a twinge of pain and guilt flash through Maya. What had it been now? Five months since she'd gone missing? Maybe more. An exact date was hard to pin down. Maya had all the details of possible sightings of her sister set down, but it was hard to work out which ones were real and which weren't.

Megan was younger than her by five years, gentle where Maya was tough, always the kind of girl who had been interested in dresses and gossip when Maya had been the one getting into fights. She'd talked about going to art school but had ended up working for a tech company instead, in human resources.

As far as Maya could tell, Megan had been going about her normal life, and she'd just vanished. It was the "as far as she could tell" that bothered Maya most, because if she'd just been there for her sister, maybe none of this would have happened. They'd been close as kids, even in the first days when Maya had joined the army. Now though, it seemed that her sister could go missing and Maya couldn't even be certain exactly when it had happened, because she hadn't been keeping track of Megan's life closely enough to know. She'd assumed that her sister was ok. Maya hated herself for that.

She sat, trying to work through the small scraps of her sister's life. When someone vanished, Maya knew that there were always the same possibilities: they'd fled to escape their lives, they'd run to escape someone, or someone had taken them.

Megan didn't have anything in her life that it seemed she might want to run from. She had a steady job, Mom said that she sounded happy when they talked, and Maya wanted to believe that her sister would have talked to her if she'd been in any kind of trouble.

Maya sat for half an hour with her laptop, linking up to law enforcement databases to check through the latest scraps of information. There was pitifully little that was new. Instead, Maya worried at the old information. She had the forensics report from Megan's apartment, and went over it, hoping to find some sign of something out of place.

She thought about motives, but Maya had a hard time believing that *anyone* could have a motive to take her sister. Megan was a good, kind, generous person, and as far as Maya could see, the people around her loved her. She was single, with her last serious boyfriend a few months before she vanished.

Maya had seen the worst of what people could do to one another, over and over. She'd seen families left without answers for years, and people who disappeared, never to be found.

Every crime Maya solved made the world a little more like it should be, but it didn't find Megan.

Dead or alive, she was going to find her sister. Maya wasn't going to give up, even though months of searching had so far turned up precisely zero useful leads. Maya wanted to be able to put together a theory, but there just wasn't enough to go on.

She'd tried looking for possibly dangerous casual boyfriends, and there weren't any. She'd explored the possibility that Megan had stumbled into something dangerous at work, but there didn't seem to *be* anything dangerous to find. Maya had talked to their mother, and neither of them could think of a single reason why someone would have wanted to take Megan.

Maya kept looking until she couldn't stand it any longer. Too much of this would drive her mad. Plus, she'd finished her juice. She needed a break.

Not able to think of anything better to do, she decided to walk down and collect her mail. She took the steps slowly, her mind still trying to chew over her files in the hope that there was something that might lead to her sister. Maya tried to console herself with the idea that no body meant that there was still hope Megan might be alive, but the experience of her job told her how easily a body could be hidden or lost.

She made it down to the mailboxes, set on one wall outside the super's office. Maya used her key to unlock hers and took out the usual thick bundle that gathered when she'd been away. She moved over to a trash can, sorting the pile into things she might want to read, and things that could go straight in there.

Bill... takeout menu... store card offer...

Maya sorted through it, most of what she held dropping straight into the trash. When she got to the postcard, she almost dropped it in with the rest, assuming that it was probably some promotional thing. Still, she stopped short. What if *this* was how Megan chose to get in touch, saying that she was having a great time in Goa or somewhere? Ok, maybe not that, but what if it was from some family member wanting to get in touch, or a friend?

The picture was of cute bunny rabbits gamboling in a meadow. It didn't seem like the sort of thing anyone she knew would send Maya, but still, it was kind of cute. There was a return address for an Anne Postmartin on the top. Maya frowned, because she didn't know the name. Was this just the marketing department of some company after all, trying to catch her attention? Yet the postcard was handwritten, and that alone was enough to make Maya read.

Instantly, her blood ran cold.

I have taken twelve bunnies for my own. Twelve lovely lost women. You have a chance to win them back from me, a reward for services to be rendered. There are crimes that must be solved. Your first is contained here.

Maya stared at it, trying to make sense of it, even as it felt like a yawning pit was opening up underneath her. This didn't happen. Questions flashed through her. How had someone managed to find where she lived? Was this serious, or just some sick joke? Did someone really have women locked away somewhere?

Every instinct she had said that this was real, and that made a feeling of dread start to flow through her.

Still, she managed to think like the agent she was. Holding the card carefully by the edges so that she wouldn't compromise any fingerprints, Maya read on.

There are rules. You have until 12 midnight on the 29th.

The 29th was just a few days away. Midnight to do what? There were no details set down. Was this all meant to be some kind of puzzle?

Succeed, and a bunny goes free. Fail, and a bunny dies.

Maya's first instinct was that she would use the time to find whoever had sent this message and make them pay, but it seemed they'd anticipated that.

Try to find me, and a bunny dies. I will be watching.

Maya tried to think, but she couldn't think, because of the one word at the bottom, signing off the rest.

Sar-bear.

Maya dropped the postcard in shock, caught it, and stared at it again, willing that final word to say anything else. It couldn't be right. It… no, she couldn't believe it. Yet it was there, set down, as clearly as the rest of it. A word that made her heart pound in her chest and made her feel almost sick with fear.

That word… that was the nickname Megan had given her as a child, and had only used when they were alone. The only way someone could know that was…

Was if they'd taken her.

CHAPTER THREE

Maya read the postcard, over and over, as if doing so might somehow change what it said. A part of her hoped that if she read it enough times, she might be able to get control of the sudden surge of emotions threatening to overwhelm her. She felt confusion that something like this could be happening, tangled up with anger that anyone would do something like this.

Fear for her sister made up most of it, though. Did someone really have Megan? Were they really holding her and threatening to kill her unless Maya… what? Solved a bunch of crimes for them? It sounded impossible. It sounded like the kind of thing that no one would do. If they wanted an old crime investigated, why not just contact her office?

The improbability of it all made Maya wonder if this might be someone messing with her. Could this all be some big hoax, designed to make her life hell for however long it took to find out what was going on? Maya had seen hoaxers and timewasters on investigations before. Maybe this was just another one?

Yet even as she thought it, she knew that was mostly what she was *hoping* was true. She hoped that this was just some badly judged idea of a joke, because then her sister wouldn't be in danger, and nor would eleven other women. If she could tell herself that this was some attempt to get in her head, then Maya could start to slow down her pounding heart and get enough control to think.

There was the nickname, though: Sar-bear. Maya tried to tell herself that anyone might have guessed that, that it was a pretty obvious nickname given her name. It was only obvious with hindsight, though. If someone were to hear that it was the nickname her sister had given her as a kid, then it made sense; but to guess it? It didn't feel likely.

Did that mean that someone definitely had Megan? Maya tried to tell herself that it could mean something else. Maybe Megan had just mentioned it to whoever had sent this. In theory, it could even be Megan doing this, trying to scare her for not being there for her. Maya couldn't believe that her sister would do that, though, and she didn't think Megan would simply tell someone the nickname, either. It had been a private thing, just for the two of them.

Maya realized that she'd been standing, just staring at the postcard for several minutes now, paralyzed by the enormity of what was happening. She was reacting like a civilian, not a trained federal agent. It was time to change that. If Megan was in danger, then she needed to act.

Her hand went to the butt of her gun, and Maya went outside, checking up and down the street as if she might be able to spot whoever had sent the postcard. Maybe she would. They'd *said* that they would be watching, after all. Maya scanned the street, trying to see if anyone was watching, but the problem with that was that *of course* people were watching. She'd just run outside with her hand on her gun.

Stop reacting, she told herself. Think.

She rushed back upstairs to her apartment, and the first thing she did was to dig through her office until she came up with a roll of evidence bags. Maya deposited the postcard in one, determined to protect it from further contamination even if its journey through the mail had probably already wiped away most of any evidence that was on it.

Once she'd done that, Maya grabbed her keys, her weapon, and her jacket. This might be someone just messing with her. If so, Maya would find them and make sure that they didn't do something like this again.

If it wasn't some sick joke, though, her sister was in danger, and the only hope Maya had of getting her back was the resources of the FBI. She had to get back to work right away.

*

Maya drove back to the FBI headquarters faster than was probably safe. Her head told her that an extra few miles per hour wouldn't make a difference right now, but her heart overruled it. Every moment she wasted now was another moment that her sister was in danger.

This wouldn't have happened at all if Maya had found Megan earlier. If she'd found some clue before now, she could have gotten her sister back safely, and none of this would have happened. Now, she felt like she had to make up for that, whatever it took.

She parked and rushed up into the building, all but running to get through the security checks as quickly as possible.

When Maya reached the bullpen, Harris was out on the floor, making his way around the desks as he checked on the progress of cases. He was currently talking to Agent Ignatio Reyes, a Latino man in his mid-thirties, with a lean physique and a serious expression. It only grew more serious as Maya rushed over there, with the postcard in its evidence bag held out for Harris to take.

"Read this," Maya said. "Right now."

"Hey, Gray," Reyes said. "I know you're the hero of the hour, but I have cases too. You want the boss, wait your turn."

"I thought I told you to take the day off, Gray," Harris said.

"Sorry," Maya replied, "But this is life and death. Harris, just read it."

There was no time for niceties when twelve lives might be at stake. The urgency of it must have shown on Maya's face, or perhaps Director Harris just trusted that she wouldn't do something like this without a reason, because he took the postcard and started to read it through the plastic of the evidence bag.

Maya watched the way his expression changed, with the initial flare of disbelief followed by growing seriousness.

"This could just be a sick joke," he pointed out, still staring at the card.

"Can we afford to take that risk?" Maya asked.

She saw Harris shake his head. "No, you're right. If there's even a chance that this is real… we have to take it seriously."

"There's more than a chance," Maya said.

Harris looked up at her. "What makes you so certain?"

Maya took a breath. There was a danger in telling Harris the next part. What if he didn't want her anywhere near all of this, because her sister was involved in it? What if he decided that the potential for it to cloud her judgement was too great?

Maya knew she had to risk it. If the FBI didn't take this seriously because she held back, then Megan could be in even more danger.

"The name at the end is a nickname that my sister used to call me," Maya said, wincing at giving away something so personal. "A *private* nickname."

Maya took in the surprise on Harris' face.

"Your sister? The one who's missing?" he said.

Maya nodded. "I only have one sister. And this nickname means… it means some madman might have my sister as a captive, along with eleven other people," Maya said.

"Mad *woman*," Harris said. "There's a return address with a name. Whoever this Anne Postmartin is, she's been pretty careless."

"It has to be a fake name," Maya said, although there was something about the name that was faintly familiar. "No one would be stupid enough to send a threatening postcard with their name and address on it like that."

"Never underestimate the capacity of people to do stupid things," Harris said. "We catch people because they make mistakes."

Maya had to agree with that, even if she didn't see as much of it in her job. The ones who made such big mistakes probably found themselves caught long before they made it to being cold cases.

"O'Keefe!" Harris called out, and Maya was glad that her boss was acting so decisively on this. She tried to tell herself that they would find answers. They would find her sister.

"Sir?" A younger man looked up from his desk.

"Take this postcard down to forensics. Get them to pull prints, DNA, anything they can get."

"Yes sir," the agent said, and took the evidence bag.

"Reyes," Harris said. "Run Anne Postmartin through our system, see if there's anything there."

"Right," Agent Reyes said, tapping in the name.

Maya could see him looking puzzled.

"Well, she's not our kidnapper," Reyes said.

"How can you be so sure?" Maya asked.

"Because Anne Postmartin is dead."

Dead. It took a moment for that to sink in. When it did, Maya understood the point of the name on the message.

"*She's* the one whose murder this bastard wants me to solve," Maya said. She looked over to Reyes. "She *was* murdered, right?"

She saw Reyes nod.

"Anne Postmartin. Lived in Cleveland. She was nineteen years old when she was murdered. Her body was found abandoned on the shore of Lake Erie. The coroner found that she'd been strangled."

"Suspects?" Harris said.

Maya saw Reyes shrug.

"There were a few who were questioned by the local PD, but there weren't any major leads to follow, everyone had an alibi, and none of the motives seemed strong enough. There was just one thing: she was killed on the night of the full moon."

Maya's breath caught for a moment with those words because she understood what Reyes was implying. If this was what she thought it was, then this was big.

20

It seemed that Harris understood as well.

"The Moonlight Killer?" the Director said.

Back when she'd been thinking of joining the Behavioral Assessment Unit, trying to understand the Moonlight Killer had been a major effort.

She saw Reyes nod. "That was the speculation at the time."

"The Moonlight Killer?" Harris said. "They want you to find the Moonlight Killer? Is that even possible? We don't know anything about them for sure. Not even really how many people they've killed, because the only pattern is that they've killed all their victims on the night of a full moon. There isn't the usual obvious victim profile. We *think* they've been operating for around twelve years, but it could be longer."

"What I don't get," Reyes said, "is that this mysterious contact, who's threatening to start murdering their captives, wants you to *find* a serial killer?"

It looked that way, and that only raised more questions for Maya. Why her, for a start? Did this person think that she could somehow succeed where dozens of other investigators had failed? Or was it meant to be an impossible task, designed to drive home to Maya just how helpless she was to do anything?

Even if they were serious about Maya trying to find the truth, why would a killer care? Was this someone who had lost someone to the Moonlight Killer, and was trying to force the FBI to find them when they hadn't been able to before? Was this some rival killer, who somehow saw this as a way of getting rid of the competition?

"The question now is if we go along with this or not," Harris said.

Maya stared at him. She hadn't considered the possibility that he might not want to.

"I think this is a serious threat," she said. "If there's any danger that the person who sent me this card will actually kill someone if we don't investigate, then I think we have to at least try to solve Anne Postmartin's murder."

"Or we find the one who sent this before they have a chance to make good on their threat," Reyes suggested. "Sir, I'd like to volunteer to lead a team to find the sicko who sent this. Even if they're watching Gray, we can still find them."

The thought of doing that made Maya feel sick. "I want him found, too. Of course I do. But we have to tread carefully. If there's any sign of an investigation, you could be putting all of these… these 'bunnies' in danger."

"All of them, or just your sister?" Reyes asked. "You're too close to this, Gray. You can't make rational decisions about it."

Maya gave Harris a pleading look. If he shut her out of this, she wouldn't be able to do anything but sit and wait in the hope that the others there would be able to find Megan before it was too late. Maya wasn't sure that she could stand that idea. No, she *couldn't* stand it. She wasn't going to let it happen.

"Sir," she said. "Let me investigate this. Let me try to find Anne Postmartin's killer."

"You want to find the Moonlight Killer, when no one else has?" Reyes asked. "Gray, you're good, but do you know how arrogant that sounds?"

"About as arrogant as thinking that you can find *this* guy without any risk to twelve hostages," Maya shot back.

"Enough," Harris said. He stood there, seeming to consider it. "I've made my decision. We're going to take this seriously, and for now at least, we're going to go along with what the message wants. That buys us time to try to find whoever sent it via whatever the forensics turn up. Gray, you'll head up the investigation to try to find Anne Postmartin's killer."

"Sir-" Reyes began, but Harris cut him off.

"Gray is the best cold case investigator we have. However close to this she is, she's the one with the best chance of finding the truth."

Maya felt more gratitude towards her boss right then than she'd felt before in her life.

"Thank you, sir," she said. "I won't let you down with this."

"Don't thank me yet," Harris said. "You still have to actually do this."

Maya swallowed at that thought. That was the catch with all this. Harris might think that she could do it, and whoever had sent the postcard clearly thought that she could, but there was a world of difference between that confidence in her and actually solving a crime. The sheer scale of what Maya had to do next started to sink in for her then.

She had to do what so many had failed to do before her. She had to find the Moonlight Killer.

CHAPTER FOUR

Maya saw the glistening expanse of Lake Erie in the distance, so vast that it was more like flying towards the ocean than towards just a lake. She could see Cleveland there on the edge of it, its skyscrapers sticking up like jabbing fingers, the signs of its heavy industries there in the factories and plants on the edges. To Maya, it looked very different than Washington's classically inclined public buildings and carefully planned layout. It looked a little flatter and a little more sprawling to her, like a limpet clinging to the edge of the lake.

Maya had spent the flight to Cleveland going over the details of the case, determined to hit the ground running once she landed. There wasn't any time to lose, when her sister's life hung in the balance.

That was the reason she'd taken a flight, too. Normally, Maya liked the control that came from driving herself where she could, but now, she couldn't afford to waste the extra hours.

The plane came in to land, and Maya disembarked as quickly as she could, using her badge to rush through the procedures at the other end. A message on her phone caught her eye, from Harris:

Cleveland PD will be sending an officer who worked the original case to meet you at the airport: Detective Spinelli. He'll be showing you around on this. No arguments.

It took Maya a moment to realize why he'd included those last two words: Harris had effectively found a way to saddle her with a partner for the duration of this, even if it was only some member of Cleveland PD, and not a fellow FBI agent. Since Maya would need every scrap of information she could get if she was going to solve this before the deadline, she couldn't even find a way to ditch him.

Maya found herself picturing Detective Spinelli, her mind's eye conjuring up some grizzled veteran who'd been on the police force forever. Maya found herself picturing a fat older cop who'd seen too much and had lost whatever drive he'd had when he joined up. She amused herself by picturing him balding and pinch faced, plodding and barely competent at his job.

A part of her even hoped that he was, and not just for the usual reasons that most of her peers in the FBI looked down on those who hadn't wanted to join the more prestigious agency. Maya was hoping that, if the local PD had missed the Moonlight killer only because they were incompetent, then that might mean there was some glaring piece of evidence that she could spot to catch him out.

Maya made her way out into the parking lot, trying to spot anyone who might be Detective Spinelli. She couldn't see anyone who looked like the fat, aging cop of her imagination.

"Agent Gray," a voice said, and Maya spun to find herself facing a guy who *definitely* didn't match that description.

He was probably her age, with the tapered physique of a swimmer. He was better looking than any cop had a right to be, with clean shaven, chiseled features, dark hair that was only just starting to get a little too long, like he'd forgotten to get his regular haircut, and the most piercing gray/blue eyes Maya had seen up close. His physique was hidden by the cut of his suit, but Maya was still sure that it was pretty much a wedge of lean muscle. As tall as she was for a woman, he was still a head taller than her, probably six four or six five. Maya caught the bulge that denoted a shoulder holster and saw the flash of a badge half hidden by his jacket. *This* was the cop she was meant to meet?

"You're Detective Spinelli?" she asked. Maybe they'd substituted the old cop of her imagination for some newcomer to the department.

"That's me," he said. "Call me Marco."

"*You* were on the Anne Postmartin case?" Maya asked. She realized how that had to sound, like she didn't believe him. The only thing was that she wasn't sure if she did. "Sorry, it's just that you seem too…"

Too something. Too clean cut. Too much not the image that Maya had formed in her mind.

"I was there. I'd have thought you'd want to get to your hotel first. Or are you that eager to catch the Moonlight Killer?"

There was an edge of something there: a kind of resentment. Detective Spinelli didn't sound happy to have the FBI there. Maya decided that keeping things professional was the best way to go.

"Can you show me where the crime scene was?"

"All right," Marco said, and led the way to a beat-up old Explorer, so rusted out on one side that Maya found herself wondering if it was safe to get in it. She did so anyway, stowing her bag in the back.

"You know," Marco said, "you still haven't told me your first name."

24

Maya thought about telling him that "Agent Gray" was fine. That would probably be the best reminder of why she was there, and of the fact that she was running this investigation. On the other hand, it was usually better not to alienate the local cops quite so early in an investigation.

"It's Maya," she said.

She wasn't going to give him more than her name, though. She found that it was generally better not to give away too much. If the events of the last day or so had proved anything, it was that *any* personal connection could be used against her.

They started to drive, and Maya watched Cleveland go past as Marco drove. It was a lot more industrial than Washington, but then, what wasn't? Maya saw factories and workshops passing by. Since it was getting into evening, a lot of them were closed anyway, but Maya caught the realtor signs that showed where some wouldn't be opening up for business again.

"Tell me about the case," Maya said to Marco, because hearing it from one of the original detectives would give her far more than just looking at the files. She'd looked through them on the flight, but this would let her know what he and the others had considered important, and where there still might be room to find out more.

"Anne Postmartin," Marco said. "Nineteen years old. Found strangled on the shore of Lake Erie, in Edgewater Park. On the night of the full moon."

Maya had to shake her head to stop herself from imagining Megan dead there, by the water's edge. She had to focus on Anne, and not just for the best chance of saving her sister. The dead deserved every effort she had to try to bring their killers to justice.

"What about Anne herself?" Maya asked.

"She lived at home with her parents," Marco said. "She was taking some courses at a local college, getting decent grades, but not outstanding ones. The area where she really excelled was in dancing. She won titles for it. Her parents tried to explain it all to me. They were so proud of her."

Maya had never been a dancing kind of girl as a kid. That had been more Megan's thing, and even she had given up ballet when she'd hit her teens.

"What about friends, boyfriends?" Maya asked.

"Anne was a popular kid," Marco said, taking a turn in the Explorer. "We talked to a couple of her previous boyfriends, but they had alibis for the night of the murder. We talked to her friends, and they couldn't think of any reason why anyone would want to hurt her. She was taking part in a dancing show down by the shore of the lake."

All of those sounded like promising places to look for clues.

"We were still looking into all that when people started getting obsessed with the Moonlight Killer," Marco said.

Maya caught the note of bitterness there.

"You don't think it was the Moonlight Killer?"

"I don't know," Marco said. "But I *do* know that once people started chasing after him, I didn't have a chance of looking at anything else. Are *you* just here to hunt the Moonlight Killer, Agent Gray?"

Maya thought about that. She'd assumed when the postcard had come that the kidnapper wanted her to catch the Moonlight Killer, but the postcard hadn't said that, had it? The kidnapper wanted her to solve the crime, that was all.

"I'm here to follow the evidence," Maya said. "Whichever way it leads."

Marco looked pleased by that. "Really?"

Maya nodded. "I want to solve this. Anne Postmartin deserves justice."

And it was the only way to save her sister.

She saw a hint of tension go out of Marco's posture. She hadn't realized that she'd been watching him so closely.

"That's good," he said. "That's… very good."

They turned a corner and reached Edgewater Park. There was nothing like this in DC. It was a huge expanse of greenery hugging the shore of the lake, with trees in woodland clusters and large open expanses of grass, all wrapped around a beach front. Maya could make out plenty of people out on that beach front, even now. That made her wonder how easy it had been for a killer to strike and get away without being seen.

They pulled up and walked down towards the beach, with Marco leading the way. They passed couples getting out picnic baskets, a couple of people carrying canoes, and plenty of people who were just there to laze on the beach. Even though Maya wasn't wearing an FBI jacket, she was sure that she and Marco stood out, when everyone else was in swimwear, and they were walking along in their suits.

Maya followed Marco, towards a spot where the beach met a stand of trees. Even walking up to it, Maya could see that it was a more secluded part of the beach, and she guessed that in the trees, anyone there would be practically invisible to others.

When Marco stopped, it was so abrupt that Maya had to keep herself from walking into him. Although given the muscles of his physique, she would probably bounce off him. He gestured to a patch of beach in front of them, broken up by occasional rocks, then to the trees behind.

"This is the place where Anne Postmartin's body was found, but forensics found plant matter on her clothes, suggesting that she was killed in the trees," Marco said.

Maya considered that, staring at the shoreline. She didn't know what she expected to see. It wasn't like showing up at a fresh crime scene, where there was still a chance to find evidence.

Just looking at this place told her *something*, though. There was a direct line from the trees to this spot, and rocks at the far side of the trees meant that it would have been hard to go that way. Someone could come that way alone, but to go back with a body would be impossible.

"Whoever killed Anne dragged her here to dump her in the lake," Maya said. "Do people go into those woods?"

"Sometimes," Marco said. "It's kind of a meeting spot for kids and couples."

So someone didn't want Anne found that quickly, or maybe they wanted the lake to wash off evidence. But then, Maya wondered, why abandon her at the edge of the lake? Could they have been interrupted before they could finish? Did they just underestimate how hard it was to move a body? Maya had no way of knowing, but either way, it didn't seem as clean and professional as it might have been with the Moonlight Killer.

The more she saw of this, the less she thought it was him.

"Maya?" Marco said, snapping her out of her thoughts.

"Yes?"

"I was asking if you needed anything from me?"

Maya tried to think. Some things were standard, but the way each case went was different. Then there was the question of how much she wanted someone tagging along with her.

"I want to hear anything you know that *didn't* make it into the files," she said. "The stuff you told me before was great, but it's in there. I want to go over the files with you in case you remember something new. Where the original investigation found witnesses, I want to reinterview them, just in case they've remembered anything new. I also want to take a close look at anything that got swept aside because it didn't fit the Moonlight Killer theory. I want to be thorough about this."

"I can help with that," Marco promised her. "But can I ask something? Why you? Why now?"

Maya thought about telling him all of it, about the postcard, and about her sister. It probably made sense to share information with the local cops where it was relevant. It was only the briefest of thoughts, though. This was her investigation, not theirs, and if she started to talk about her reasons, they might have the same reservations that Reyes had brought up back at the office. Only this time, there wouldn't be Harris stepping in to overrule them.

No, it was better to keep that side of things quiet.

"I investigate cold cases anyway," Maya explained. "But now, we think that this might be related to other murders, and we want to make sure either way."

It was kind of a non-answer, and from the look Marco gave her, with a quick glance of those gray eyes, it was obvious that he caught it.

"Ok," he said, although from his tone, it clearly wasn't. "Where exactly do you want to start, Agent Gray?"

Maya thought for a moment or two. There were plenty of choices, plenty of people they could talk to and places she could look. Maya knew that she needed to start with the heart of this, though, with the people who knew her best.

"Anne lived at home, right? Then I want to talk to her parents."

CHAPTER FIVE

When they pulled into a street lined with cedar trees, Maya found herself staring, trying to guess at the life Anne Postmartin had lived before her death. The houses were painted each in a different color and the lawns were neatly kept. It looked like one of those middle class, not quite affluent enough for a mansion but still doing ok, kinds of places, where the cars on the driveways were mostly pretty new, and everything was carefully maintained.

Maya could make out the twitch of a few curtains as people watched them pull up. That suggested that this place was quiet enough that people noticed visitors.

"Take it easy on them," Marco said. "They've been through a lot."

They walked up towards the door of the house they'd come to visit. Even as they did so, it swung open.

It revealed a man in his forties, with features creased by worry, dark hair just starting to turn grey around the edges, and a slightly stooped posture. He was wearing a suit, like he'd just come home from an office. This, Maya guessed, had to be Jon Postmartin, Anne's father. He looked like he was in shape, but Maya could see that his hair was far from perfectly clipped, and his suit didn't quite fit him perfectly. That suggested someone who worked out because he needed the effort of it, or to distract himself, rather than someone who was doing it for appearances. His watch and shoes looked expensive, but the shoes were scuffed, and far from polished. Maybe this was a man who once had cared about that kind of thing, but the death of his daughter had changed that about him.

"It's good to see you again, Jon," Marco said, and Maya was impressed by the warmth he managed in that. Maya wasn't quite sure what to make of Marco, this cop who didn't look like she expected, who thought that this old case of the Moonlight Killer's *wasn't* down to the infamous serial killer.

"I wish I could say the same," Jon Postmartin said. "Tami is in the lounge. You'd better come through."

He led the way inside, and there, Maya had the impression of a home kept as pristine as possible through near constant cleaning. The walls looked freshly painted, the carpets were spotless, and every hint of metal shone. As they went through into the lounge, Maya took in the standard catalogue furniture, the gray painted walls, and the utter neatness of it all. There was a large TV on one wall, but Maya was more interested in the trophy cabinet, containing a collection of medals and cups that would have shamed most high school track stars. There were pictures in there as well, of Anne Postmartin smiling onstage, or on podiums. To Maya, it seemed like this one corner of the room had been given over to the memory of the Postmartins' daughter, while the rest had been carefully scrubbed clean of anything that might bring them pain.

Tami Postmartin sat in the exact center of a cream leather sofa, and to Maya it looked as if she'd carefully composed herself the moment she and Marco arrived. She sat up perfectly straight, wearing a dark skirt and a teal blouse. Her blonde hair was cut shoulder length, and Maya could see echoes of Anne Postmartin's fresh-faced prettiness in her features, but that was diluted by a tension that obviously came from Maya being there. She saw Jon Postmartin move to sit beside his wife, just as carefully upright, reaching out to take her hand even as he nodded for Maya and Marco to take a seat on two armchairs.

"Tami, Jon," Marco said, "I'm sorry to have to come round like this, but we need to talk to you. This is Agent Gray of the FBI. She deals with cold cases."

"The FBI is reopening the case?" Jon asked.

"We are," Maya said. She kept it neutral, not wanting to give any hint of the reasons she was there.

"Why?" Tami asked. "I'm sorry, I know how that sounds. It's just… why now?"

"Why now, when we're just starting to put all this behind us?" Jon put in.

It wasn't the first time Maya had heard a reaction like that. She didn't enter investigations in the first big push to catch a perpetrator, when everyone was rushing to help at once. She got there after time had passed, when people were trying to move on with their lives, and even local law enforcement were too focused on more recent cases to enjoy committing resources.

Maya considered the best thing to say. She couldn't tell the truth about her sister, not here like this. She suspected that simply saying that she was reviewing the case wouldn't be enough, so what did that leave?

"Anne's killer is still out there somewhere," Maya said, not seeing another good option.

She saw Tami Postmartin wince at that.

"The Moonlight Killer," she said. "It's always about *him*."

"It's about your daughter," Maya promised her.

"Really?" Tami said. "Because at the time, it didn't seem like it. All the press who came just wanted to talk about that... that *monster*, never about our daughter."

Maya could understand that, too. The press always seemed to give killers more attention than their victims. How would she feel if this were Megan, and all people talked about was the person who had taken her?

That also gave Maya a way in, though.

"Why don't you tell me about Anne?" she said.

Even then the Postmartins looked uncomfortable.

"It will help," Marco put in from the side. "The person who killed your daughter is still out there. Anything you can tell us might help us catch them."

That was a bit too quick, a bit too much pressure, for Maya's taste. She'd been trying to build up gently, but Marco would have brought them straight back to thoughts of the killer. Maya tried to signal for him to calm things down, but the problem with having worked with someone for literally an hour was that there wasn't enough time to get to know one another so that kind of thing worked.

"Let's just focus on Anne," Maya said. "What was she like?"

"She was wonderful," Tami said. Maya could make out the tears at the corners of her eyes. "The best daughter anyone could ask for."

"She loved to dance," Jon said. His face was a mask, hiding his emotions where his wife couldn't hold them back. "She won so many competitions."

"And she had a job down at a dance show near the beach?" Maya asked, remembering the detail from the casefile.

"Yes," Tami said, looking suddenly proud. "As part of Lucas McFadden's dance troupe. All her life, she'd talked about being a dancer, and here she was getting paid to do it."

She got up off the sofa, leading the way to the trophy cabinet, and even though there were still tears in her eyes, Maya could see the pride starting to win out against them as Tami pointed to one of the trophies, a small one towards the back.

"That was the first one she won, when she was just five years old. This is a picture of her when she first got into the McFadden School of Dance. These are the medals that she won in-"

"Tami," Jon said, "I'm pretty sure that the agent doesn't want to hear the complete history of our daughter's dancing."

"It's ok," Maya said, with the most reassuring smile she could manage towards Tami. "The more I know about Anne, the better. Tell me about the people close to her. Who were her friends?"

"Oh, Anne had so *many* friends," Tami replied, sounding as proud of that as she had of the dancing. "She was such a popular girl."

"Anyone in particular?" Maya asked. It wasn't just idle curiosity. She'd seen the place where Anne had been killed. What would it have taken to get her to walk into those woods with someone? She would have had to trust them, and that meant one of the people she already knew.

"Oh, half the neighborhood would have been there," Tami said. "Plus a few kids from school. I can give you their names, if you like?"

"That would be good," Maya said. She started to make a list while Tami talked.

"There was Kai Jones, Petra Martin, Suzie... what was her last name, Jon?"

"I don't think it matters, Tami," Jon said. "I doubt the Moonlight Killer is one of Anne's schoolfriends."

Maya looked around. He didn't look happy about any of this, his posture tense and his hands working at one another.

"I know," Maya said, "but it would help if I could get a full picture of Anne's life. Did she have any boyfriends?"

The names of a couple were in the file, but Maya asked anyway. Partly, she did it to see if there were any more, but she also wanted to see how much about that side of her daughter her parents knew.

"There were a couple in the past: Lucas Crain and Justin Longson," Tami said. "I don't think Anne was seeing anyone when she... when it happened."

That fit with what Maya had heard.

"Who else would have been at the performance on the beach?" Maya asked, trying to draw things back to the night of the performance. Already, though, she suspected that it was going to result in too large a group of potential suspects to really narrow things down.

"Well, our neighbors," Tami said. "That would be Edward and Justine on that side, and Adam and William on that one, although they moved to Wisconsin, so they aren't there anymore."

Maya nodded at that. It was another thing she was used to with cold cases. With standard investigations, everyone was still more or less where the crime had taken place and leaving in a hurry was a sign that the FBI should look closer. With cold cases, people moved away, sometimes even just to get away from the memories of the crimes near them.

"Her dance coach, Lucas McFadden, of course," Tami said. "And everyone from the academy. Lots of people."

Too many people to work through, at least before the deadline. Ordinarily, the one thing Maya had on her side was the time to be methodical. Now, the enormity of the task in front of her hit her all at once.

Maya looked back towards Marco, and she didn't know if she was looking for some kind of reassurance or not. It sounded stupid, given that they'd only just met. Maybe, she decided, she was just hoping that he would take over for a moment or two while Maya collected her thoughts and stopped her heart from pounding at the thought of how little time she had.

This time, Marco seemed to take his cue better. "And of course, the two of you were there as well to see your daughter dance."

"That's right," Tami said.

Maya found her eyes on Jon, though. Some of his composure seemed to be starting to slip, his hands moving faster against one another, like they were trying to wash one another. She knew when someone was agitated, when they wanted to say something, but didn't think that they could.

"What is it, Jon?" she asked. "What aren't you saying?"

"Nothing," Jon said, quickly. A little too quickly.

It was obvious to Maya that he was hiding something, but what? More than that, how hard could she afford to press? Maybe another time she would have taken this slowly, but now, with so little time, Maya knew that she couldn't afford to wait.

"I can see that there's something," Maya said. "Please, anything you can tell me will help."

"It's nothing," Jon said, half standing and then sitting back down again, like he'd almost been ready to walk out of the room.

33

"It doesn't *look* like nothing," Maya said, trying to be as sympathetic as possible. "Jon, Mr. Postmartin, please. Anything you can tell me might be important."

"Agent Gray," Marco began. "Maybe we should give Mr. Postmartin a minute?"

Maya ignored that attempt to get her to back off. As much sympathy as she felt for the Postmartins, she knew that she couldn't let this go. There was something here, and Maya wasn't about to let it go if it might let her find the answer in time to save her sister.

"We'll take a break soon," Maya said, trying her most calming voice. "I promise. I'd just like to know what it is about the night of the dance show that has you so upset, Jon."

"It's... I... I argued with her! Is that what you want to hear?" Jon Postmartin demanded. "The last thing I said to her was..."

"What was it, Jon?" Maya asked, switching to a softer tone. "What did you argue about?"

"I..."

Maya watched Jon Postmartin start to break down, his composure falling away as he sat on the sofa, his posture collapsing in on itself. Maya felt bad for him in that moment, and a little guilty for having pushed him like that, even though there was a chance it might get her answers.

"She always worked so hard as a kid. The dance show was proof of how well she was doing. Anne was going to win the regionals, then the nationals!" Where before he'd barely looked at the trophy cabinet, now he beamed at it with pride.

Maya thought she understood, then.

"You put a lot of effort into helping her get better," Maya guessed.

"I drove her to every class," Jon said. "I was there when she wanted to do extra practice. I never had a son, but I decided that I was going to take her dancing as seriously as I would have if a son wanted to be the best at baseball or football."

Maya had heard about that kind of driven parent, determined that their child would be the best. She knew that people would probably call *her* driven, but that had always come from within herself, not from outside.

"What happened, Jon?" she asked, sympathetic now.

Jon Postmartin seemed almost physically pained by that. "Just lately, she'd seemed less... focused. I could see her chances at the nationals slipping. I suggested that once she'd done the show down by the lake, she should come back and run through her routine again."

"Anne didn't like the idea of having to do the extra practice?" Maya asked, as gently as she could.

"Ordinarily she would have been the one suggesting it!" Jon Postmartin said, like he still couldn't understand why his daughter wouldn't want to. "She was always the one suggesting going through steps after a performance, wanting to make everything perfect."

Maya wondered to what extent that was true. Maybe Anne Postmartin *was* the one driving that, or maybe she'd been trying to live up to what her father hinted was the right thing to do. Maya didn't know the dead young woman well enough yet to judge it, but she was determined that she would. In a cold case, Maya always wanted to know the victim better than they knew themselves.

"What changed?" Maya asked, still keeping her tone soft.

"I don't know," Jon replied. "She started going out without saying where she was going. She wouldn't concentrate while she was working out. And then this. She said that she wanted to go see her friends after the show."

That sounded to Maya like a perfectly normal thing for a young woman to want, yet at the same time, any change in a victim's routine might mean something. For someone who normally wanted to do nothing but practice to suddenly want to see friends might hint at something more, something worth looking into.

"How did you react to that?" Maya asked. She was trying to be as sympathetic as she could. She knew how painful these memories had to be.

"I told her that she ought to practice, with nationals coming up," Jon replied.

"And what did Anne say to that?"

"That she… that she was a grown woman, and she could do what she wanted. Then I told her that she would follow my rules while she lived under my roof."

Maya guessed that wasn't all of it. "And how did she react?"

"That if that was the problem, she didn't have to keep living here," Jon said. Maya could see the tears streaming down his cheeks now. "The last things we said to one another, and it was an argument. I thought it would blow over. I thought it would be fine, and then…"

And then his daughter had been killed, leaving no chance to say any of the things he wanted to say. No chance to make things right. That

35

was one of the cruelest things about murder; it took away chances from everyone it touched.

"She stormed off," Jon said. "I could have followed, but I didn't. I… I'll never forgive myself for that."

Tami put an arm around him then, but Maya could see the surprise on her face. It seemed Jon hadn't even told his wife about the argument.

"Can either of you remember any other details about that night?" Maya asked. "Anything at all?"

"Anne… Anne had a backpack with her when she left," her father said. "She grabbed a few things to take with her when she went."

Maya thought back to her look through the files on the flight. "What was she wearing when she left? Do you remember?"

"I'm not sure," Mr. Postmartin replied.

"A white crop top and a dark skirt?" Maya asked.

He shook his head. "I… no, I don't think it was that. No."

That had been what Anne had been wearing in the crime scene photos, which meant that Anne had changed at some point before her death. She'd dressed up after the performance, not just changed back into casual clothes.

Maya took out a business card, setting it down on the arm of the couch.

"You've been very helpful," she said. "If you think of anything else, anything at all, please call me anytime."

As they left, Marco gave her a puzzled look.

"What was all that about the clothing at the end?"

"I have a hunch," Maya replied. "But we're going to have to talk to Anne's friends to find out for sure."

CHAPTER SIX

At Maya's insistence, they arranged to meet Amber Wellsey and Kristen Evens in a café near the local college. It seemed best to her to meet them in a place where they would feel comfortable, and she suspected that meeting them there would help to remind them of Anne.

"So, tell me about them," Maya said, as she sat with Marco. She'd seen what was in the file, but anything Marco could remember on top of that might help.

"They were two of Anne's closest friends," Marco said. "We questioned them in the initial inquiry, because in that first phase, we talked to as many of the people around Anne as possible."

Maya believed that. From what she'd seen of Marco, he was a thorough cop, and he'd clearly not been as fixated on the Moonlight Killer as a lot of other people.

"What I don't get is why you want to talk to these two," Marco said. "There's no reason to think that they had anything to do with Anne's death."

"I don't think that they did," Maya assured him. She'd seen the files. Neither Amber nor Kirsten had any reason to kill Anne, and they both had alibis in any case. "But I think that they can tell me things about Anne that someone else might not be able to."

"Such as?" Marco asked. He took a sip of his coffee.

"Such as why she changed her clothes on the night of her murder," Maya said. It was such a small detail. Anne had been at the dance show. She'd been in her costume for it, but she hadn't changed back into the clothes that she'd been wearing that day. Instead, she'd changed into the clothes that she'd been found in. Was it just a whim, or did it mean something more?

Maya had to hope that it meant more.

Amber was the first to arrive. She was short, dark haired and brown eyed, wearing jeans and a sweater. To Maya, she looked in shape, and also nervous, like she wasn't sure what this was about. She had a bag over her shoulder, with a book under her arm that seemed to be for calculus. Maya guessed that she might have come from the college library. From the tired rings under her eyes, Maya guessed that she'd been there a while, maybe writing a paper?

Kristen came in on a moment or two after her. She was slender, with short, spikey hair dyed a deep red. She was wearing workout gear, but Maya could see a flash of cloth that seemed to be a store uniform of some sort poking out of the tote bag she was carrying. Maya guessed that she was juggling dance practice and work in between her classes.

The strangest thing about looking at them was that, in spite of being twenty-one, Anne had looked barely more than a kid. A couple of years on, and her friends were fully grown adults. It was one of the strangest things about working cold cases; she got to see how other people moved on and aged while the dead never would.

"Thank you both for coming," Maya said, standing. "Can I get you anything? Coffee?"

"A chai latte, please," Amber said.

"Just black coffee for me," Kristen said.

Maya got them, bringing them back and sitting with the young women. Amber looked nervous, as if she thought she might be in some kind of trouble. Kristen looked like she wasn't quite sure what was going on.

"You want to talk to us about Anne?" she said. "That's what you said on the phone, right?"

"I do," Maya said. "I'm Agent Gray. This is Detective Spinelli. He worked on the original investigation."

"I remember him," Kristen said.

Amber nodded. "I mean, he's pretty memorable."

Maya could only agree with that sentiment, and then had to remind herself that she wasn't some twenty-something who could be so easily distracted. She had a job to focus on.

"I want to start by saying that you're not in any trouble," Maya said, and that seemed to relieve some of Amber's nervousness. "I'm just looking to get as complete a picture of Anne and her life as I can."

"Ok," Amber said, "but I'm not sure what we can tell you, right Kristen?"

Her friend nodded. "We told the police everything we knew at the time."

Maya was used to that response, but she also knew that people could sometimes remember things that they hadn't, even years previously. Sometimes, it could even just be that they were finally ready to say something they'd held back, the way Jon Postmartin had

38

been. Even if it proved to be some small detail, it would still be something.

"That's ok," Maya said. "I just want to understand what Anne was like. How long did you know her?"

"Forever," Kristen said. "I used to go to the same dance classes as her, and Amber knew her from school."

Maya saw Amber nod.

"We met in Mrs Temsci's English class," Amber said. "We had lockers next to one another in high school."

"In the dance classes, she was amazing," Kristen added. "She was always the best girl in the class. I used to wish I could dance half as well as her."

Briefly, Maya considered the possibility that Kristen might have been jealous of Anne, but it didn't sound like that. It sounded more like admiration. She could see the young woman swallow, trying to hold back her emotions at the memory of her friend.

She saw it, and it seemed that Marco did too.

"It's ok," he said. "We know it's difficult. We won't keep you any longer than we have to."

He looked over to Maya, and she knew that he still couldn't see the point of all this. He seemed to be letting her run with it, though. He trusted her enough for that, at least.

"It sounds like you were close," Maya said. "It says in the files though that you hadn't seen as much of her in the days before her death?"

"I saw her at the mall a couple of days before the show, but only for a short time," Amber said. "She wanted to buy some clothes, but then she had to go. She was so busy, I barely got to talk to her."

"It was the same for me," Kristen said. "I saw her at the show, obviously, but even then, it was like she was somewhere else in her head, you know?"

"What do you mean?" Maya asked. This was the difference between files and talking to people. A file could give her facts but talking to Anne's friends could tell her far more about what Anne had been thinking and feeling at the time of her murder. "Where do you think she was?"

"I'm not sure," Kristen said. "I think maybe she was just so focused on the nationals that everything else kind of fell away for her."

That didn't quite fit with the argument Anne had with her father shortly before her death. Maya knew that she had to dig deeper, but she had to be careful about it.

"What was it that made you think that?" Maya asked. "Was it something specific that Anne said or did?"

"She was always training," Amber put in. "Even from when we were kids, she would only be able to hang out some of the time when she had a competition coming up."

Maya saw both Amber and Kristen start to nod, but she wanted to delve into what had been different this time. Everything that had happened at her parents' house convinced Maya that *something* had been unusual.

"But she was always there for you, normally?" Maya guessed. "She managed to make time for you?"

"Usually, yes," Kristen said. "We'd hang out on weekends. We'd find time in her training schedule. We'd hang out at college."

"But not in the days before her death?" Maya asked. "Did something change?"

Kristen paused, obviously trying to think. "I guess. It was just the nationals, though. We'd go to class, and I'd want to hang out afterwards, but she'd always have to stay for extra training, you know? Or she'd have to go in to train when we wanted to hang out during the day."

"The nationals sound like a big deal," Maya said. "What would it have meant for her to go there?"

She didn't know about dancing, but she could guess at how important something like that might be to her. She'd *seen* how important it was to Anne's father.

"She could have had a career as a dancer," Amber said. "Even if she didn't win, just being able to say that she went would have been enough."

Kristen nodded. "She could have won, too. I couldn't watch the competition for so long afterwards, because of..."

Amber reached out and put a comforting hand over hers.

"But you watched it back later?" Maya asked. "It's ok if this is too hard."

"I watched a video of it online," Kristen said. "She was just *better* than all the ones who were there. She could have won it. I have to believe that. And now, every time *I* dance, it's like, I know that I'll never be as good as she was, but it's like she's there with me."

40

Maya could appreciate that sentiment.

"It must help, feeling that," she said. "And I'm sure she'd be happy you were keeping going."

"I hope so," Kristen said.

"Were you in the show that night?" Maya asked the young woman. Kristen nodded.

"So you saw Anne in the show, on stage? Did you see where she went afterwards?"

"No," Kristen said. "I'm sorry. I keep feeling like, if I'd insisted on hanging out with her, or if I'd just gone with her-"

Maya knew how she felt, because she was currently feeling pretty much the same. If she'd just been with her sister, then she could have stopped someone from taking her. Could have stopped all of this from happening.

"This isn't your fault, Kristen," Marco said. "There was nothing you could do."

Maya wished that she could believe that was true for her too, but she couldn't, even as she knew that it had been the right thing to say. Why hadn't *she* said it? Because she'd been too busy focusing on her sister to say the obvious thing, the *right* thing.

"Detective Spinelli is right," Maya said. "This is the fault of whoever did this, not you, or anyone else."

There was one more thing that Maya wanted to ask then, the thing that had meant she'd needed to find some of Anne's friends in the first place.

"Now, I spoke to her parents," she said, "and it occurred to me that there might be some things that parents wouldn't know, but her closest friends might."

"Such as?" Amber asked, looking puzzled.

"Well, if she had a boyfriend, would she tell you? She'd want to gossip about him with you, right?" Maya said. "She used to talk about boyfriends with you in the past?"

"Always," Kristen said. "Anne could always get any boy she wanted."

"Not that she did," Amber added quickly. "But when she had a boyfriend, she used to get so excited."

"And did she have a boyfriend back then?" Maya asked. "One she didn't tell anyone else about?"

41

Each of the young women looked at the other, as if to check whether Anne had told one of them without telling the other, but then they shook their heads almost in unison.

"No, she didn't say anything to me," Kristen said.

"Me neither," Amber agreed.

Maya felt her heart sink at that. She'd had so much hope that this hunch might pay off, and now, it looked as if it wasn't going anywhere. There was always a kind of frustration that came when a suspicion didn't pan out, but now it was a hundred times worse, because she'd used up time that she didn't have in checking it.

"Thank you both for coming here," she said. She passed them both her business card. "If you think of anything else, no matter how small, call me."

Maya kept her composure while she watched them leave. It seemed that Marco was watching *her*, though.

"What was all that with the boyfriend?" he asked.

Maya did her best to explain, even though it felt as though her idea had been shot down already.

"Anne was going somewhere, and it wasn't to extra practice. Somewhere she cared about enough to have an argument with her dad about it even though she was clearly serious about dancing. She got changed specifically to go to the stand of trees where she was killed, into nice clothes. *Date* clothes. To me, that says that she was slipping away to meet a boyfriend."

Maya saw Marco tilt his head to one side. "I don't know, Maya. It seems a little thin."

"If there was a boyfriend no one knew about, and Anne went to meet him," Maya insisted, "then he could have killed her there, left no signs of a struggle, and no one would know."

"Except that the two friends who knew Anne best say she didn't have a new boyfriend," Marco pointed out.

Maya sighed, feeling deflated as she did it. "Except that, yes. And her two most recent boyfriends that we know about have alibis."

"But you still think it's worth looking into, don't you?" Marco said.

"I…" Should she just let this go and move on to the next thing? No, there was something to this. Why had Anne behaved as she had if not for that? "Yes, I think it is."

"Then I'll make some calls and see if anyone else has heard of a boyfriend no one else knew about," Marco said.

Maya felt her eyes widen slightly in surprise, and Marco obviously caught her reaction.

"What?" he said. "I want this guy caught as badly as you do."

No, not as badly, because Marco wasn't the one with a life hanging in the balance. Even so, Maya felt more grateful than she might have imagined that he was willing to go the extra mile on this.

"In the meantime," Maya said. "I want to get back to your office. I want to go through everything again and make sure we haven't missed *anything.*"

"There might be something," Marco said. "We kept paper versions of the files, including the thoughts of the others on the original investigation. I can drag them up, if you really want to go through it all."

That sounded perfect to Maya. If there was something in those files, it might help to blow this whole thing wide open. It had to, because little by little, she was running out of time.

CHAPTER SEVEN

The local precinct was a low, squat building that looked to Maya as if it had been there forever, with the whole neighborhood growing up around its crumbling brickwork. It seemed to Maya as if someone had tried to renovate it recently with a lot of modern glass and steel, but the renovations hadn't really done anything to transform the crumbling heart of it. She found that she liked that.

When Maya went inside with Marco, it was like stepping into any one of a dozen other local precincts that she'd been in while looking at cold cases. They always had the same smell of sweat and anxiety, always had the same constant noise that came from bringing in street level perps. She found herself longing for the officious quiet of the FBI headquarters, even as she stood there, taking it all in.

"This way," Marco said, leading the way through the place. "My boss has set aside an office for you."

"He wants me where I can't get in the way of real policework?" Maya guessed, only half a joke. From the slight look of discomfort on Marco's face, she knew that she'd guessed right.

"Sorry," he said. He actually sounded as if he meant it, which was something.

"I'm used to it," Maya replied. "No one wants the FBI around, especially not someone working cold cases."

Marco looked over at her, and Maya thought she saw some sympathy there as he led the way up a couple of flights of stairs.

"How did someone make detective and stay so innocent when it comes to the politics of all this?" Maya asked.

"Maybe it's because I don't care about the politics since I'm a good detective?"

"Maybe," Maya agreed.

Marco certainly seemed like a committed detective, and he was obviously good with people. Maya certainly *hoped* that he was a good detective, if he was going to help her with this.

Instead, she went through the bullpen of the precinct, which was far busier and more chaotic than her department at the FBI.

"This is us," Marco said, opening the door to an office that was clearly mostly a place for the department to store its junk. "The files should be in here somewhere."

Maya saw filing cabinets around the walls that looked like no one had touched them in years, a desk that had a file propped under one corner to stop it from wobbling, and a couple of chairs so rickety looking that she was almost afraid to sit in them. The evidence board had scribbled reminders about things that Maya guessed had happened months back at least. The glass windows made it a goldfish bowl, where everyone could look in at her, but she couldn't do anything to interfere with the business of the department. It was about as clear a statement that the local chief didn't want her there as she was likely to find.

"Sorry," Marco said again. "A couple of the other guys... well, they don't want anyone making them look bad."

"It's fine," Maya said, and forced herself to take one of the seats in spite of her misgivings.

"I'll try to dig out the files," Marco suggested.

"That would be good," Maya agreed. It had been a long day so far, but she was determined to keep going. She should go back to her hotel, but the more of a head start she could get on the case, the better.

While Marco went to the abandoned filing cabinets, Maya got up and found the drawstring for the office blinds, pulling them down, then used her laptop to call up the FBI files on the Moonlight Killer. If there wasn't a clear thread making it certain that the murder had to be someone Anne Postmartin knew, then Maya had to take the possibility of it being the Moonlight Killer seriously.

She started to read over the files, wanting to make sure that she had everything, because that would give her the best chance of spotting the way any evidence fit into the pattern later on.

Marco came back, setting down a collection of files that gave off a cloud of dust as they landed. "How much do you know about the Moonlight Killer?" she asked.

She saw Marco make a face. "I very briefly had to become an expert, when no one would let me look in any other direction two years ago."

Maya tried to imagine what that would have been like, being pushed into one line of inquiry when you wanted to look elsewhere. She guessed it had to be frustrating, even though she'd never had it

45

happen. One of the many good things about working alone was that she could look where she wanted to look.

Maya wasn't about to stop doing that now.

"Then tell me," Maya said, sitting back from her computer.

Marco stood there and recited the facts almost by rote.

"The Moonlight Killer has almost twenty murders ascribed to him. The first killing attributed to him is a schoolteacher named James Sanders, ten years ago, but there could be more, from earlier, that we simply haven't picked up. The murders are spread across the country, with no obvious geographical pattern. There was also a pattern in the MO of the crimes, with his preferred method being strangulation with a thick rope."

"Mostly, but not always," Maya countered. "There have been cases with manual strangulation, too."

Which brought them back to the one part of this that *was* consistent.

"Every killing," Marco said, "took place on the night of the full moon. The profilers and the rest spouted theories about how it's significant to him in some way, either in a reference to the tradition of madness being linked to the full moon, or just because some significant event in his life happened then. Did I miss anything, Gray?"

Maya paused. She could tell how frustrated Marco was with all of this, but they needed to keep an open mind. If this was the Moonlight Killer, then they were potentially chasing after a very dangerous man, someone they couldn't afford to take lightly even for a second.

Still, she knew that it would help if Marco was on her side for this, and there were definitely other avenues to explore. Besides, it would be foolish not to consider *every* possibility.

"Ok," she said. "Then let's focus on what we *haven't* both heard before."

She started to read through the files Marco had brought. "We know that Anne Postmartin was strangled on the night of the full moon, probably by hand, according to the coroner's report."

That took some of the edge out of Marco's posture. He was clearly happier discussing this now that she wasn't just assuming that it was the Moonlight Killer.

Now that she wasn't trying to prove anything to Marco, Maya pulled out the coroner's report and read through it.

"There was no sign of DNA under Anne Postmartin's fingernails, and the evidence from around the bruises on her neck suggests that the killer wore gloves." Maya looked over at Marco expectantly, to see if he would get the significance of that.

He frowned slightly. "It feels like you're back to telling me what we don't know."

Maya shook her head. "This *does* tell us something. Gloves? In the summer? Someone came prepared, which means this wasn't a spur of the moment thing. It wasn't some drunk guy who followed her from the show, made an unwanted advance and then strangled her. It was planned. There's no evidence of a struggle, or of Anne trying to run. That suggests either she knew whoever this was well enough to let them get close, or they got the drop on her so completely that she didn't have time to react. Then there's the way her body was left by the water. When I first heard that, I thought it was a typical serial killer display of their victim, but when we went to the shoreline, it looked more like the kind of place where someone might have been trying to drag Anne's body into the water, but then had to abandon her when they heard someone coming. Then there's this business with the boyfriend who no one knows about. If we knew one existed, he'd be my prime suspect right now, but without him… I don't know."

"So are you saying it's the Moonlight Killer or aren't you?" Marco asked her.

"I'm not sure," Maya said. "But there are inconsistencies. There are things that point to someone who planned what they're doing, and there are others that suggest either someone Anne Postmartin knew, or someone without any experience of killing, or both."

Maya kept going through the file, and she saw the notes from the original investigation, about the suspects they were considering, the possible avenues of investigation.

"There are notes here about looking at Anne's family, her former boyfriends, her dance coach, her friends," Maya said. Looking through, she could see some basic interviews with them, and a few alibis established, but no more than that. "None of those lines of investigation went further?"

"No one was interested once all the talk was of the Moonlight Killer," Marco said.

Maya got up and started to write things on the evidence board, doing her best to erase the notes that had been on there so long they'd more or less become permanent. She divided it up into two sections. One, she labelled MK, with the initials of the killer. The other, she labelled UP.

"UP?" Marco said.

"Unknown perpetrator," Maya said. "All the evidence for the Moonlight Killer goes on this side. All the evidence that it could be someone else goes on the other."

Maya started to write. On the Moonlight Killer side of the board, she put the words "Full Moon", and "Carefully Planned", then added "Strangulation" after a moment or two of thinking.

"Why the hesitation?" Marco said.

"If it had been with a rope, I wouldn't have," Maya said. "That's so obviously the Moonlight Killer's MO. And it's still strangulation. There are several other cases of manual strangulation that have been put down to him. It's just not as common."

She wished that she didn't feel so uncertain about all this. It would all be a lot more straightforward if she could just come down on one side or the other of this case. If she knew which avenues of investigation to pursue, that would give her a clear idea of where to look for evidence next, and it was her best chance to resolve this quickly.

Before a woman was killed. Before her *sister* might be killed.

The impact of that thought was as great even now as it had been the first time Maya had thought it. The fear was there, threatening to overwhelm her, forcing her to concentrate on her breathing to quiet it.

Maya didn't *feel* fear like that, not normally, not ever, that she could remember. She hadn't felt it in the midst of rocket attacks and firefights back in the army. She hadn't felt it like this facing down even the toughest criminals. There had been fear in those moments, obviously, but it hadn't been this paralyzing thing, threatening to overwhelm her.

"Are you ok?" Marco asked.

The reason was obvious to Maya: it was about Megan's safety, not hers. Worse, it was something that might be out of her control. She didn't know if there *was* any new evidence to find in this case, or even if the kidnapper would give Megan back once Maya did what he wanted.

"Gray, are you ok?" Marco repeated.

"I'm fine," Maya lied, because the alternative was telling him about her sister, and she couldn't do that. She wouldn't do that. "Just thinking about the case."

48

Marco gave her a look that said he didn't believe it, but Maya had stared down professional interrogators in training. She could manage a poker face with one good looking cop.

"Seriously, I'm fine," she said. "I'm just tired after traveling so far."

Eventually, he stopped staring and relented.

"Ok," he said. "I'll leave it. What goes on the 'not the Moonlight Killer' list?"

Maya took another moment to collect herself. She had to force herself to focus on the case, and not on everything that she might lose if she got this wrong.

"The lack of a struggle," she said. "The way the body was left. The change of clothes. The change in Anne's behavior before the murder."

She put them up on the board. Neither was definitive. It was possible that the Moonlight Killer had simply struck so swiftly that Anne Postmartin hadn't had time to react. It was possible that he'd been disturbed while trying to display her body by the shoreline, rather than someone else being disturbed while trying to make the body disappear. Both of those things were possible, which left Maya with the same problem as before.

"So which way do we go with this?" Marco asked. "Which way do we look first?"

Maya knew without asking that he would want to come down on the side of it not being the Moonlight Killer, just because of the way he'd had to chase after FBI investigators hunting that particular ghost before.

Maya didn't have the luxury of being wrong, though. Noon on the 29th, that was her deadline, just days away. There wasn't enough time to conduct a thorough investigation into both possibilities. There was barely enough to look at one the way she would have wanted.

The kidnapper had to know that. Was this pressure, this feeling of not having enough time, this fear of getting things wrong, a part of his sick game?

"Which way, Maya?" Marco asked again.

The more Maya looked, the more she realized that, practically, there was only one answer.

It wasn't just that the evidence seemed to come down marginally in favor of a killer close to Anne Postmartin. There was also the simple fact that dozens of people had already tried and failed to catch the Moonlight Killer. Chasing after him was a recipe for using up all the precious time they had before one of the kidnapper's "bunnies" found herself murdered.

Maya couldn't allow that.

"The best way to make progress is to look at the avenues that haven't been explored," she said, trying to make it sound like it was a simple, logical decision and not something that made her heart tighten with the fear that she was making the wrong choice.

"So we keep looking at the people close to Anne?" Marco said.

Maya nodded. She'd decided it. For better or worse, their course was set. "We'll interview as many more as we can and try to find new evidence. Maybe if someone thought that they'd gotten away with this because everyone was looking at the Moonlight Killer, the very fact that we're looking will shake something loose."

"So where do you want to start tomorrow?" Marco asked.

Tomorrow? The part of Maya that could feel time slipping away in the case wanted to do this right now, regardless of how late it was.

The rest of her could feel how exhausted she was, though. It was probably only the coffee that was keeping her going at this point. She needed to think to solve the case, and for that, she needed to sleep.

"We've already spoken to her parents and her friends, so let's try the next most important person in her life," Maya said.

"One of her ex-boyfriends?" Marco said.

Maya shook her head. "She was trying to be a professional dancer, Marco. I want to talk to her dance coach."

CHAPTER EIGHT

The McFadden School of Dance wasn't at all what Maya had expected when they arrived the next morning. The one time Maya had gone along with Megan to a dance lesson, it had been in a tiny studio over a Chinese restaurant, accessible only via a metal fire escape.

This wasn't anything like that. It was a big, glass fronted academy, so that Maya could see a couple of young women moving through dance steps under the direction of a middle-aged man in workout clothes. A large sign over the door proclaimed it to be "Cleveland's no.1 dance academy! The home of champions!"

"It's a bigger deal than I expected," Maya said as she and Marco stepped inside.

She took in the reception area, with its rows of seats for parents and students to wait, its pictures of beaming dancers standing on stages and podiums. Most of the dancers were girls and young women, although there were plenty of older photos of a handsome young man caught in mid leap upon the stage. Maya spotted a couple of clippings alongside, giving rave reviews for Lucas McFadden's performances.

This was him, then, or had been. He'd been a very good-looking young man, with high cheekbones and a muscular physique shown off by the tightness of his dance outfits. Maya spotted a couple more photos of the same man, a couple of years older, beaming with his arm around dancers as they held up trophies.

"He's serious about this being the home of champions," Marco said, nodding towards the spot where a row of trophies sat on shelves, declaring victory after victory in dance competitions.

There was no one around that Maya could see to run the reception desk, which seemed a little surprising given the scale of the place. She could hear Ravel's Bolero coming from the dance studio, at a volume that made it hard to concentrate.

"Do we wait?" Marco asked, gesturing towards the chairs and a few dancing magazines set out there that Maya guessed were to keep parents occupied while their children were in classes.

Maya considered that. Waiting would be the polite thing to do and would probably make it easier to talk to Lucas McFadden. At the same time though, Maya couldn't shake the feeling that every moment spent waiting was a moment wasted, a moment that she might need to solve all this before the deadline. She'd barely slept. She certainly couldn't just sit and wait while Megan was in danger.

"No," she said. "My guess is that Mr. McFadden will have classes all day. If we don't interrupt, we'll never get a chance to talk to him, or we'll have to waste the whole day before we do."

"You're that eager to make progress?" Marco asked, with a glance at her. "What is it? You need to get back to DC?"

"I've only been given a limited time here," Maya said. It was true, as far as it went. She didn't like holding back the full truth from Detective Spinelli, but she also knew that the moment she told him, she'd be off the case. "I'm on a deadline."

She heard Marco sigh. "Then I guess we interrupt."

Maya knocked on the door to the dance studio before she entered. As she did so, the two young women she'd seen dancing through the window came to a halt, relaxing even though the music was continuing. The middle-aged man who had to be Lucas McFadden had his back to the door, so it took him a moment to register that Maya and Marco were there.

"Why are you stopping, girls? Your auditions are in two weeks. We need to get you ready."

"Excuse me," Maya said, trying to keep the interruption as polite as possible.

When Lucas McFadden turned, some things were exactly the same as they had been in his pictures. He had the same high cheekbones, the same strong, handsome features, even most of the same muscles. Maya could spot differences, though, in the very slightly receding hairline, the hair that was only dark because it was kept carefully dyed, the very slight softening of his features from living well. She could see the spot where his fake tan ended at his neckline, in a line of lighter skin. He was still good looking, but it was an older, more carefully constructed thing. Maya guessed that he was the kind of guy who still thought of himself as in his prime despite hitting his forties, and who was determined to eradicate any evidence to the contrary. She saw his eyes flick over her and Marco, then flick away just as fast.

"What are you doing in my studio?" he snapped at them. "I'm in the middle of a coaching session."

"I'm sorry to just come in," Maya said. "But there was no one at reception."

52

"I sent Marcy off to run some errands," Mr. McFadden replied. "But I'm in the middle of a session right now. If you're here to ask about couples' ballroom lessons, I have some slots in the Thursday night class. Seven thirty. Now, out with you."

Maya tried to imagine herself and Marco ballroom dancing together, him in a tuxedo, and her in... what? Some sequined ballgown? The idea was almost enough to make her laugh, even if the thought of dancing that close to Marco did have a certain appeal that Maya had to shake off with a reminder that she was in Cleveland on business that might mean life or death.

"Agent Gray, FBI," Maya said, flashing her badge. "This is Detective Spinelli of the Cleveland police department."

Maya saw the look of worry that flashed across his face, mixed in with irritation and something else she couldn't place.

"No, no, it's still no," McFadden said. "I have no time."

"This is important, Mr. McFadden," Maya said.

"Important? Do you know what important is? Important is dance competitions coming up and no time to prepare! Important is young lives being shaped, and that shaping being interrupted because of... what is this even about?"

"We'd like to talk to you about Anne Postmartin," Marco said, from beside Maya.

"Anne?" McFadden said.

A part of Maya wanted to ask if he thought they were there about something else, but she guessed that doing that would only serve to alienate him further. Instead, Maya tried her best smile.

"We're reinvestigating her death," she said. "And since you were her dance coach, we'd like to ask you a few questions, see what you remember."

"This still isn't a good time," McFadden said. "And I don't want to go through all of this right now, when Emily can't even get her arabesques right! If you wait until my receptionist gets back and then make an appointment..."

"Please, Mr. McFadden," Maya said. "It won't take long, and I'm sure you want us to catch Anne's killer as much as everyone else."

"Yes, of course I do," the dance instructor said. He still looked frustrated, but at least he gestured to the door. "Let's go out to the waiting area. Girls, run through the steps on your own."

They went out and took seats out in front of the reception desk, with Marco and Maya sitting across from Lucas McFadden.

53

"You're really bringing all of this up again after so long?" the dance instructor said. "Anne's parents have just been starting to come to terms with things."

"You're still close with Anne's family?" Maya asked.

"Anne was my star pupil," Lucas said. "More than that, she was like a daughter to me; she was here so much. To have to go through all of this yet again is just... it's too painful."

Maya could see that pain etched into his expression. She could definitely hear how little Lucas McFadden wanted them there. She had to tread carefully.

"I don't want to cause you any more pain," Maya said. "But it's important that we do everything we can to try to find Anne's killer."

"And you think I can help with that?" Lucas asked. "I told the police everything I knew at the time and..."

Maya saw him look more closely at Marco.

"Wait, you were there, weren't you?" Lucas said. "Which means you've heard everything I can tell you already."

"I was on the case," Marco said. "But now we're pursuing new avenues of investigation."

"What new avenues?" Lucas demanded. He seemed quite agitated to Maya now. "What could there possibly be that's new after two years? What did you miss?"

Maya thought she saw Marco flinch slightly at that, and she realized that he'd probably been asking himself exactly that question since Maya had shown up wanting to reinvestigate this case. What must it feel like for him, wondering if he'd missed something crucial?

Maya knew that she had to focus on Lucas McFadden, though, and what he knew.

"You're coming in here as if you're magically going to solve everything, and as if I and my students must drop everything for your convenience!" Lucas snapped. "Why are you wasting my time like this, when I've said it all before?"

"I would still like to hear what you have to say," Maya said. "The better the picture I get of Anne and of that night, the better chance we have of finding the truth. Can you tell me about her?"

"What do you want to know?" Lucas retorted. "She was a very special young woman. She was going to be a champion, a star. I trained her from when she was young, and I have never seen anyone else with that kind of promise."

"She was in a show down by the beach the night of her death?" Maya asked.

Lucas nodded, looking suddenly proud. "A grand extravaganza, designed to show off the talents of those of my pupils who made our school's troupe. Anne was the star of the show."

"So you saw her during the show, because you were there?" Maya asked.

"Of course," Lucas said, in a tone that made it clear he thought it was a stupid question. Maya was just getting started, though.

"What about afterwards?" Maya asked. "Did you see her then?"

Lucas looked a little uncomfortable at that question. "What do you mean, Agent?"

"Did you see where she went, or who she spoke to?" Maya asked.

"I'm sorry," Lucas said, "I can't help you. I had so much to do, supervising things with the performance."

"I understand," Maya said. She took a moment before asking her next question. It didn't follow naturally from the last, but sometimes that was a good thing, teasing at all the strands of a thing until she could find a clear direction. "Do you happen to know if Anne had a boyfriend at the time of her death?"

"A boyfriend?"

It was a second or two before Lucas answered. Maybe he was just trying to make sense of the sudden question, or maybe he was trying to wrack his brains, to remember.

"No," he said at last, "If she had a boyfriend, I didn't know anything about him."

"That's all right," Maya said. "And in the days before her death, leading up to the performance, she was doing a lot of extra training, right?"

Lucas frowned. "Actually no. She even missed a couple of sessions, which was most unlike her. Normally, she was my little star, but I actually had to remind her about the importance of being there for training then."

Maya looked over to Marco, and he gave her the same look. This was something new, something they hadn't heard before.

"Do you know where she was during those sessions?" Maya asked.

"No, why would I?" Lucas replied.

"So you didn't check when she started missing sessions?" Maya kept going.

"I assumed that she simply needed a break for a week or two, and then things would be back to usual."

That was interesting. Anne's friends had been sure she'd been avoiding spending time with them to do extra workouts. This, though, fit more with what her father had said about her not wanting to do extra training.

She'd had something else to do that had been more important to her, but what?

"Can you tell me where you were the night of the murder?" she asked. "What you were doing after the show?"

"You want to know if I had an alibi?" Lucas replied. Looking at him closely, it seemed to Maya that he was sweating. It might be nothing, just the aftermath of working out, but she didn't think so.

"I just want to know where everyone was," Maya said, not wanting to turn it into an accusation.

"As I said, I was dealing with the wind down of the performance. These things don't just *stop*, you know. I had to supervise the technical breakdown, and the stowing of equipment. I was with several technical crew members and volunteers the whole time."

Maya looked over to Marco and felt a note of disappointment as he nodded.

"We checked at the time," he said. "Half a dozen witnesses confirm that Mr. McFadden was there for a couple of hours after the show."

If this had been immediately after the murder, Maya might have gone back and spoken to each of those witnesses, just to be sure. As it was, after two years, there would be no way of catching any inconsistency. Lucas McFadden had an alibi that wasn't about to be broken in a hurry.

Assuming that there was anything to be broken. The dance coach might be a completely innocent man. It was just… there was something off about him, something that Maya couldn't quite place, but that made her want to take a closer look his way.

Just the way he'd reacted when they'd come in had been strange. Anyone else would have seen it as obvious that they were there about the murder, but it was almost as if he were worried about something else.

"If that will be all," Lucas said. "I don't think this conversation is adding anything I wasn't asked two years ago, and I really have to get back to my students. They are my pride and joy."

"I thought that was Anne," Maya said.

"Yes, yes, of course," Lucas replied. "But a coach must nurture talent wherever he finds it."

Maya nodded, and she and Marco walked out.

"You're *sure* there's no way he could have slipped away at the time?" Maya asked. It wasn't that far from the show to where Anne had been killed.

"His alibi looked pretty solid," Marco assured her. "You just don't like the guy."

"No," Maya agreed, "I don't."

She took out her phone and punched in a number for her office.

"FBI, Reyes speaking."

"Reyes, it's Gray," Maya said.

"How are things in Cleveland?"

"Too early to say," she said. "Can you run a background check for me? A guy named Lucas McFadden. He was Anne Postmartin's dance instructor. I want to know about him, his students, any red flags, all of it."

"All right," Reyes said. "I'll see what I can find. But don't get used to it. You've got the lead on this, but I'm not your secretary."

"Just let me know what you find out," Maya said.

Marco still looked doubtful. "I'm telling you, it's not him. Still, it's nice not to be chasing after the Moonlight Killer on this for once. Where now?"

"I think we need to work out who else might have had a reason to kill Anne," Maya said. "We need to work out who might know about this mystery person she went to meet, and we need to work out who might *not* have an alibi you already checked."

"You already know who you want to talk to, don't you?" Marco guessed.

"I have a pretty good idea," Maya said. "But first, I want to get into Anne's head. I want to see the places she hung out."

CHAPTER NINE

The man who called himself Frank sat out on the porch of his cabin, trying to feel some connection to the beauty around him. Other people said that it moved them when they stared at the mountains and trees of this place, but then, he'd always known that other people were liars.

They certainly weren't like him.

Still, he stared at it all, because maybe this time he would be able to fathom some of what other people claimed to feel. Trees spread out on three sides, with open ground on the fourth, where rabbits hopped in chaotic lives that made about as much sense to him as anyone else's. A stream lay beyond the open ground, and the mountains beyond *that*. It was a good view from which to see people coming.

He unfolded himself from the rocking chair smoothly. Frank made a point of staying in shape. His body was a tool, and he kept it as sharp as any of his knives. In his late thirties, he was strong, and fast, and flexible when he needed to be. He knew he was good looking, and he'd learned to be charming when he needed to be.

Out here, with no one around, he didn't need to be, so his face was an expressionless blank. He didn't have anyone to impress out here except his bunnies, and they never saw his face.

That thought brought a familiar itch with it, so Frank went inside. He made his way over to a corner of the cabin where a hand-hooked Appalachian rug dominated the floor. He rolled it up precisely, not wanting to leave any creases that might indicate that this was something he did regularly, and revealed a trapdoor beneath.

The space below had taken years to build, but it was worth it. Anything was worth it to give him the space he needed to do everything he wanted.

Frank made his way down a set of iron stairs, flicking on rows of strip lights that he'd had installed. In the first space there, he pulled on a mask and gloves, picked up a torch and a stun gun. He ignored the cobwebs on the walls around him, and the damp that came from being underground. If that made things less pleasant for his bunnies... well, they wouldn't have to live with it much longer.

He stepped up to the door leading to the tunnels beyond. It was a strong, steel thing, solid enough that no one would get through it without cutting gear. Frank liked to let his bunnies run free beyond, but there were limits. A dozen bunnies, all in their warren.

Frank took out his phone and took a moment to link to the cameras beyond, watching them in their identical grey jumpsuits, moving among the featureless furniture he'd provided. A couple cowered in corners, knowing what the lights coming on portended. A couple more had decided to be brave, or stupid.

Frank unlocked the door, then kicked it back, catching the first of the ones hiding close to the door with the weight of it. He stepped through quickly, jabbing the stun gun into the second, and enjoying her scream for a moment as she fell with the electricity coursing through her. The other one tried to recover her wits and throw herself at him, but he struck her with the stun gun too. She went down in agony.

Carefully, calmly, Frank closed the door behind him. He crouched by his two disobedient bunnies, holding the stun gun and letting the spark flicker.

"I don't normally bother with torture," he said. "It always seems like a poor second best. But disobedience must be punished."

He jabbed the stun gun into each of them again, watching them writhe on the floor, listening to their screams. There was a kind of excitement to it, but it was nothing compared to the pure joy that came when he ended a life.

Frank picked one of the two, grabbing her by her arm and dragging her through to a space behind another locked door. Even now, she struggled and tried to pull back, but he was stronger than her.

This space was a dome, with computer screens along one wall, each one linked to a different camera. Some showed his bunnies, reeling in the aftermath of the sudden violence, clinging to one another for comfort. More showed information: places, dates, clues. Everything he'd learned about Agent Maya Gray. Her face was on the last of the monitors, a still view taken from inside her apartment.

For now, Frank ignored that, dragging his bunny over to the center of the room.

A circle marked out by marble stood at the heart of the space, and a circular drain at the center of *that*. A ring stood above it. Taking chains from a corner, Frank secured his bunny's hands and hoisted her onto her tiptoes, above that drain.

This one was Liza Carty, a twenty-two-year-old singer who had just signed a major deal when Frank had taken her. Her blonde hair was tangled around her round face from the time she'd spent down here, and she was crying now from the pain he'd inflicted on her, and from her fear.

Frank didn't care about either.

"Please let me go," she said, because she still didn't seem to understand how this worked. "Whatever this is, I haven't done anything to you."

"You tried to escape," Frank said. He turned Liza carefully, so that she faced the one other accoutrement of the room: a large digital clock readout, counting down.

"What... what's that for?" Liza asked.

"That is for a little game I'm playing," Frank said, although there was nothing little about any of this.

"You're going to kill me, aren't you?" Liza said.

"That remains to be seen," Frank replied. "You see, there is someone else I need to do something for me. An FBI agent. She is looking into an old murder. I want the truth to be told."

"You've done all of this to get someone to chase a murderer for you?" Liza said.

Frank allowed himself a shrug. Such physical reactions were things best used in measured ways, but here, he suspected it would seem less frightening, less cold.

"She might not have looked at this otherwise," he said. "Now, she has an incentive."

"I'm meant to be an incentive?" Liza said. "But I don't even *know* any FBI agents."

"That doesn't matter," Frank said. "She will still move heaven and earth to find the truth now. Before the time is up."

"What happens when the time is up?" Liza asked, as if she couldn't already guess the answer.

"That's when I kill you," Frank replied.

He'd put the rules in place now. It was better to stick to such things. It was better if Maya understood that he was serious.

Frank felt that he could use her first name by now. After all, he knew almost everything about her.

That knowledge gave him confidence that she would succeed. That she would bring killers to justice who otherwise might escape it. His methods to force her into it might be unorthodox, but Frank had no doubt that they would prove effective.

And if they didn't, he would give her a reminder of the stakes they were playing for.

CHAPTER TEN

Maya walked through the food court of the mall and stared in mild disbelief as Marco brought over what appeared to be two hot dogs with fries scattered on top of them the way another vendor might have scattered onions.

"This," he declared, as he reached their table, "is a Cleveland Polish Boy. If I let you come to Cleveland without trying one, I'd be failing as a host."

Was that the role he saw himself in, Maya wondered. Host, tour guide, partner? Was he determined to show off his city as well as helping her to catch a killer?

"Thanks," Maya said, taking hers and starting to walk.

"So explain to me what we're doing here?" Marco said.

"I told you, I want to get into Anne's head. I want to go where she went. I want to see what she saw."

"By going to the mall?" Marco said, with a note of disbelief. "At least the food is good. Try it."

Maya did, and she had to admit that it was a lot better than the idea of it had seemed. She took a second bite, her tastebuds not quite believing it with the first one.

"Ah, we have a convert," Marco said.

Maya made herself give a noncommittal shrug. "It's all right."

"All right? It is a work of art and you know it, Gray."

Was this what it was like having a partner, Maya wondered. She liked the camaraderie of moments like this, and the fact that he knew the case meant that it was proving useful having him around. She had to admit it didn't hurt that Marco was easy on the eyes, as well.

"What are you thinking about?" Marco asked, at the one moment when Maya knew that she couldn't actually explain the last thought she'd had.

"Just the case," she lied. "I'm trying to work out the best way to make progress from here."

"Now that our first two leads are dead ends, you mean?" Marco asked.

He didn't sound any happier about it than Maya felt. She'd been convinced, was still convinced, that Anne having a new boyfriend fit her behavior in the days leading up to her death. That didn't help them, though, if they couldn't find any evidence of who that might have been, or even that he really existed.

"I want to be certain about the boyfriend idea," Maya said. "You went through all Anne's social media when the case started, right?"

"Obviously," Marco said. "It's just standard, these days."

Standard that in the world they lived in, the first place to look for a killer was online.

"I want us to go through again," Maya said. "It's possible that while everyone was looking for signs of a killer, they might have missed something pointing to a boyfriend."

"Ok," Marco said. "We can try it. What about the dance coach?"

Maya wasn't sure what to make of Lucas McFadden. She was still certain that there was something off about him, but if Marco said that he'd checked Lucas McFadden's alibi for that night and it had held up, then it was hard to keep him as a suspect.

That left her with two leads that she didn't want to let go of, neither of which had any evidence to back it up.

It was time to find more.

"This is the mall Anne would have gone to, right?" Maya asked, as she kept walking. Around her, the crowds of older folk and kids parted to let the two of them through.

Marco nodded. "So her friends said at the time."

Maya tried to get a sense of Anne from the mall, tried to think herself into the shoes of a young woman her age. What had been important to her? Dancing, according to everything Maya had heard. So what could have been important enough to make her miss classes?

She was just back to where she'd started.

"We'll think of something," Maya said, aloud, because she had to believe that. They would find a way to solve this before the deadline, whatever it took.

"You sound very sure," Marco said.

"One of the things I learned in the army was that when there's a mission to complete, you get on and complete it. There's always a way."

"What was it like for you in the army?" Marco asked, sounding suddenly interested.

It was only then that Maya realized that she was straying into personal territory. The postcard and the threat to her sister had shown Maya just how easily any personal information could be used against her, yet now, it felt like she didn't really have a choice other than to tell Marco *something*.

In any case, it was a chance to learn more about him in turn. Maya found that she wanted to do that. That was almost as strange. Normally, so long as the people around her kept out of her way and let her do her job, the details of their private lives didn't come into it. In fact, Maya usually felt that she was better off not knowing. With local cops, when she would be gone as quickly as she came, it was usually better not to even start to build up connections with them. It was safer that way. It meant nobody could hurt her.

"The army was tough," Maya said, "but I liked the discipline of it, and I liked finding out that I could still think even when things were getting bad."

"You saw action, then?" Marco said.

Maya nodded. "Afghanistan. Iraq."

Just two words, but they carried with them a host of memories. She'd seen things that she'd hoped never to see: squad mates torn apart by IEDs, civilians killed by sniper fire. Just the thought of it was enough to bring back the smell of burning that came after an explosion, and the screams of the dying.

"It sounds like a lot to go through," Marco said.

Maya shrugged that off, because the alternative was talking about it, and that was worse.

"What's the life of Marco Spinelli like, here in Cleveland?"

"Cleveland's good, once you know it," Marco said. He shrugged. "There's not much to tell about me. I grew up here in a family of cops. For a while I rebelled against it, but I always knew what I was going to end up doing."

"How did you rebel?" Maya asked. "I can't see you joining a gang."

"Joining a swim team then taking a year out to go do triathlons abroad was enough," Marco said.

That confirmed Maya's hunch from when she'd first met him.

"Your family didn't like you doing that?" she guessed.

"They thought that I was wasting time I could be using to get ahead in my police career," Marco replied. "What about you? Do you have family?"

Maya's stomach twisted at that. They were back on shaky ground again.

"My father passed a few years ago. My mother is still alive, and I have a sister."

Maya kept her tone flat for that part, making it as clear as she could that further questions about her family wouldn't be welcome. She hoped that Marco would just assume she wanted to keep things professional, and not bring her family into it. She really didn't want to explain why she was here, or the danger that her sister was in.

"Siblings can be difficult," Marco said. He'd apparently guessed that things were tricky between Maya and Megan in a far more usual way than anything to do with kidnappers and unsolved cases.

"Yes," Maya agreed.

The people who were closest were often the ones in a position to cause the most pain. A sibling could be the biggest rival, even an enemy, in the right circumstances. But that didn't apply in this case. Anne Postmartin hadn't had siblings.

Then Maya found her eyes drifting over to a group of teenage girls outside one of the clothing stores, they were jostling one another, making fun of one of their number. They were all laughing, but Maya saw the moment when one of them said something they shouldn't. Even though she couldn't hear the words over the noise of the mall, she could make out their impact in a hurt expression, a sudden turn to walk away.

If friends were close enough, they could be almost like sisters.

They'd met a couple of Anne's friends, but no teenage girl ever had just a *couple* of friends. Anne would have had a whole pack around her, some her friends, some her rivals… Maybe one more than that?

What would it have been like here, when there was a young woman who was so obviously destined for stardom, in the midst of other people who weren't quite so talented? What would it have been like for them, seeing her win competitions and get all the best roles in performances? Lucas McFadden had insisted that Anne was his star pupil, while her parents had a cabinet full of trophies.

Wasn't it possible that someone might have been jealous of that? Maybe even jealous enough to kill?

"Marco," Maya said. "I want to take another look at the dance school."

"I already told you that the coach has an alibi," Marco pointed out.

"Not McFadden," Maya said. "His students."

"His *students*?" Marco repeated, like he was trying to wrap his head around this.

"Plenty of them were up there at the lake the night of the murder for the show, and no one would have thought twice about any who showed up to watch," Maya said. "Who has the most reason to hate someone successful?"

It took Marco a moment to get it. "Someone who isn't as successful."

"Someone who thinks that it should have been them," Maya said, "and who thinks that the only reason they aren't getting the attention is because the star pupil is getting all of it."

She found herself thinking of the person who had kidnapped her sister, then. Maya had thought it, hadn't she, back when the postcard had come? That one possibility was that one killer had gotten jealous of another. That someone might resent the attention the Moonlight Killer had received and was trying to undermine his crimes.

"I don't know," Marco said. "Killing someone over dancing?"

"People kill over the things that are important to them," Maya said. "For some of the students at McFadden's school, especially the members of his troupe, I'm willing to bet that dancing is the most important thing in their lives."

"But they're all skinny young girls," Marco said. "You really think one of them is going to be able to have strangled Anne Postmartin so easily? Most of them would struggle to cut a steak, let alone strangle someone to death."

"You know as well as I do that people are capable of more than everyone thinks," Maya said. "You must have seen the things people do. Besides, you need strength to dance. And would it have been so much of a stretch for a rival to hire someone? To get a boyfriend to do it?" ·

"I thought your focus was on finding *Anne's* boyfriend," Marco said. "Doesn't going in this direction conflict with that?"

"I still think it's a possibility," Maya said. "But we don't have evidence for it. So we try something else, and a jealous rival fits."

Marco still looked doubtful, but he nodded. "So, what do you want to do?"

"We need a list of dancers who were in Anne's classes at the time. We need to go through it, find out who might have been jealous, and look closer at them."

Marco looked, if anything, even more doubtful.

"You realize that the one person who might give us that list probably isn't in any kind of mood to help?" he pointed out. "We are not Lucas McFadden's favorite people right now."

"If he's serious about wanting Anne's killer found, he'll help us anyway," Maya said. "If he has nothing to hide, he'll give us the list."

"And if he has something to hide?" Marco said.

"Then if it's not the murder, he'll give us the list anyway, just to get rid of us," Maya said. "Either way, we'll get what we need from Lucas McFadden."

CHAPTER ELEVEN

"No, absolutely not!" Lucas McFadden snapped.

This was not the response Maya had been expecting when she and Marco drove back to the dance studio. She and Marco stood in his dance studio again, and one look at Mr. McFadden's face told her just how unwelcome they were here.

"Mr. McFadden," Maya tried. "A list of students who were here at the time of Anne's death doesn't seem like a lot to ask, and it could really help us in trying to find her killer."

"No," McFadden said. "I'm not just going to hand over the details of my business, and my students, at the whim of some FBI agent."

"It's not a whim," Maya said. "This is a murder investigation, and we need-"

"If you want the private details of my students, then you will have to get a warrant," McFadden said. "I will *not* give them to you otherwise."

It was a much stronger response than Maya had anticipated, and she found that it brought out the worst in her.

"Why don't you want to help us, Mr. McFadden?" she asked, with a look around the studio towards the receptionist who worked the front desk.

She was a woman of maybe twenty, dressed in a tight dancing outfit that suggested she also took lessons there. The roots of her dyed blonde hair were starting to show, and it looked as if her nails had been freshly fixed, leaving them longer and glossier than any nails Maya had had in her life.

"It's Marcy, isn't it?" she said, remembering the name Lucas had used earlier. "Talk some sense into your boss. Tell him that if he doesn't have anything to hide here, he should just help us. Or don't either of you want us to catch Anne's murderer?"

This was too direct, too aggressive. It wasn't the way Maya would normally have handled anything like this, and it took her a second to realize why she was being like this. It wasn't just that something about Lucas McFadden set her on edge; it was the lingering sense that she

68

was running out of time. They needed that list, and every extra second it took to get it was a second less Maya had to find the killer.

"Not my business," Marcy drawled.

"You leave her out of this," Lucas snapped. "In fact, I want you to just leave. This is private property, and if you don't have a warrant, then you have no business being here."

"What is it you're trying to hide?" Maya asked, taking a step towards him before she could help herself. She knew that she shouldn't be doing any of this, but every instinct she had said that there was something very wrong about him.

She felt Marco's grip on her arm. It wasn't tight, but it was firm enough to make it clear that he wasn't going to let go.

"We need to go, Maya. He's right, without a warrant, we don't get to be here."

Maya turned to say something angry to him, but she knew he was right. There was nothing they could do there, not yet.

"Ok, ok," she said. "We'll go."

She stalked from the dance studio, out to where the Explorer sat in the parking lot. Maya leaned against it, then slammed her palm down on its roof. It might or might not have left a dent. Given how beaten up the Explorer was, it was hard to tell.

"He's really got you riled up," Marco said, as he moved around to the driver's side. "What was that all about?"

"He's hiding something," Maya said. "Why wouldn't he give us what we needed?"

"Maybe he really is just concerned about his students," Marco suggested, although he didn't sound like he believed it any more than Maya did. "Or maybe…"

He didn't seem to want to say the next part.

"Maybe he's being obstructive because I annoyed him earlier?" Maya said.

"Maybe," Marco agreed. "He really didn't like us just walking into his lesson, asking questions. We could have waited."

"I don't have time to wait," Maya said. She might not be able to explain the reason why, but she had to get Marco to understand that part.

"Because the FBI might call you back," Marco said, and Maya could hear the note of doubt there. He didn't believe her. Maya had underestimated him.

Still there was nothing to do now except go forward with the lie.

"Exactly." Maya leaned against the car and took out her phone. "Now, if Lucas McFadden wants me to get a warrant, I'll *get* a warrant."

"There might be a quicker way," Marco said. He unlocked the Explorer. "It probably won't get us as much, but it should work. Come on, get in."

*

They drove for maybe ten minutes, and Maya couldn't get Marco to explain exactly where they were heading.

"Trust me," he said, as they pulled up to an apartment block. Marco led the way to the door, then hit the intercom.

"Who is it?" a woman's voice called down.

"Detective Spinelli, Cleveland PD," Marco said. "I don't know if you remember me, Ms. West, but I spoke to you about-"

"About poor Anne, yes, I remember. You'd better come up."

The buzzer sounded for the door, and they headed inside. To Maya, the interior looked a little dilapidated, with carpets worn almost gray by constant footfalls, and floral wallpaper that had probably never really been in fashion.

The elevator was out of order, so she had to follow Marco up four flights of stairs instead, to stand outside apartment 4B. Even as she raised her hand to knock, a woman opened the door.

She was older than Maya, probably in her mid-forties, still in shape, with what Maya took to be a dancer's physique. Her hair was a bright bottle blonde, and she wore a leopard print blouse over a dark skirt, along with enough jewelry that Maya was surprised she didn't jangle when she moved. Maya had the impression of a woman who was happy to grab attention when she could get it. She also seemed pleased to see Maya and Marco, which was proving a rarity in this case.

"Ms. West," Marco said. "Thank you for letting us in. This is Agent Gray of the FBI. We're hoping that you can help us."

"Of course, of course," the woman said. "Come in. And it's Petronella. None of this 'Ms. West' business. When a handsome man calls me Ms. West, I feel like I'm turning into my mother."

Maya found herself feeling a brief flicker of what she could only describe as jealousy. Which made no sense, because it wasn't as if there was anything between her and Marco, was there?

Maya was still thinking about that as the woman showed them through to an apartment far more cluttered than Maya's would ever manage to be. There were enough tables, chairs, and assorted ornaments for two apartments. Petronella waved Maya to an armchair, while showing Marco to a couch and sitting beside him.

"So, what can I do for you, Detective Spinelli?" she asked.

"You ran the reception at the dance school at the time of Anne's murder, correct?" Marco said.

"You know I did. You interviewed me yourself. Of course, I also taught a few classes when *he* wasn't trying to do everything. This was before he pushed me out. 'Too old,' he said."

"*He* is Lucas McFadden?" Maya asked.

Petronella looked over to her as though only just remembering that Maya was there. "That's right, dear. Has he been causing trouble for you, too?"

"He's been making it hard for us to do our jobs," Maya said.

"Oh, that's a shame," she said, although she was still looking at Marco rather than Maya.

"We need some information," Marco put in. Almost instantly, with him asking it, it seemed that Petronella brightened up.

"Whatever you need, I'll be happy to help, Detective."

Maya decided to let Marco handle this. He was obviously going to get better results than her.

"We need to know who was at the studio around the time Anne was killed," Marco said. "Who was in the troupe with her, who would have known her. I know it's a lot to remember."

"I'm sure I'll be able to manage it," Petronella said. "After all, I was the one having to do all the administration in that place. I can certainly remember the troupe."

She took a pen and started writing on a spare scrap of paper. "Let's see. Lucy Adams... Avril Deshawn..."

Maya was impressed. She'd always had a good memory, but most people, and definitely most witnesses, didn't. Yet here Petronella was recalling the names of kids who had passed through the school a couple of years ago.

She kept writing for a minute or two, then folded the paper carefully before holding it out to Marco.

"There you go," she said with a smile. "That's all of them."

"You're sure?" Marco said. "It's a lot of kids to remember."

"They trained with us for years. They were like family," Petronella said. "I would remember. That's all of them."

*

Maya was getting frustrated. She sat at her borrowed desk, staring at Petronella's handwriting and starting to tap names into the FBI system even as Marco did the same with the Cleveland PD one. She was looking for any arrests, convictions, even complaints that might point to a classmate with a history of violence.

"Reia Martin," Maya read out.

"Nothing here," Marco said.

There was nothing on the FBI system either.

"This is going to take forever," Marco said, stretching out his back. He obviously didn't like being sat at a desk for so long.

"Eager to get back to the action of flirting with former dancers?" Maya said.

She wasn't sure how she felt about him flirting with Petronella, and that was odd in itself, because it wasn't like she had any claim over Detective Spinelli. They weren't anything to one another, weren't even partners, really. It was just… well, she did enjoy having him around, and she'd definitely felt *something* when Petronella had been trying her best to get his attention.

"I wasn't flirting."

"Sure you weren't," Maya said. The truth was that she was grateful, because she wouldn't have gotten the information without him.

"You'd know if I were flirting," Marco insisted.

"Is that a promise?" Maya said, without even thinking, and then cursed herself. She needed to keep things professional. She needed to get on with the work, find a killer, and get out of Cleveland without any unnecessary entanglements.

She quickly turned her attention back to the list, and as Maya stared at it, something struck her.

"There's only one male name on this list," she said. "Dane Carlucci."

"So?" Marco said. "I can't imagine that a lot of young boys are taking dance rather than football in Cleveland."

"So what was it you said before, about the girls in Anne's class probably being too skinny to even cut up their own steak, let alone strangle someone?" Maya pointed out. "Maybe the one boy in there

72

was stronger. At least run him through the system next. Maybe we can shortcut all of this."

"Ok," Marco said, although he still sounded doubtful. "But what are you going to do when this comes back... wait."

"You were saying?" Maya said. She could tell from his expression that there was something there.

"There was a complaint against Dane Carlucci," Marco said. "Harassment."

"Going to dance classes so that he could get closer to the girls he liked?" Maya asked.

Marco shook his head. "Since part of it was making threats when one of the girls looked at his boyfriend wrong, I'd say not. There's some stuff here about him throwing things around because one of the other dancers got a part he wanted in a production. He said that she would back out if she knew what was good for her."

It was a combination that suggested someone with a temper, someone who wasn't afraid of violence towards his fellow dancers, and someone who maybe had every reason to be jealous of Anne.

"Where is he now?" Maya said. "Can you run his driver's license for an address?"

"Already on it," Marco said. "It says here that he lives in Huron. It's about an hour's drive."

"Then the quicker we get started, the quicker we get there," Maya said, determined now. "I want to talk to Dane Carlucci."

CHAPTER TWELVE

It was getting into evening as they pulled up outside Dane Carlucci's house. Maya couldn't help thinking about the contrast with the Postmartins' home. That had been a quiet little place in the suburbs. *This* was an expensive apartment building, complete with uniformed security at the entrance, and not just some smiling ex-cop doing it for the cash.

No, this guy looked them over professionally, and Maya's every instinct said that he was ex-military. Maybe it helped that he'd retained the buzz-cut, but more of that was simply the way he checked them, checked their car, made it clear that he was looking for threats.

"We're here to see Dane Carlucci," Maya said. She took out her badge, and the guard looked it over.

"Is Mr. Carlucci expecting you?" the guard asked.

"No," Marco said, flashing his own badge, "but it's important. We just drove in from Cleveland."

"I'll call up, see if he will speak with you," the guard said.

Maya held back her frustration at being kept waiting like that. One look at the guard said that insisting on the importance of their visit wouldn't make any difference to him, and if they tried to push past to avoid giving Dane Carlucci any warning of their visit, he would try to stop them, cops or not.

That left waiting while he rang up to speak with Carlucci.

"Mr. Carlucci? Two police officers to see you. From Cleveland. No, I don't. Yes, I will."

He waved them up. "You can go up, but I'll tell you now that he's not happy about having you here."

"And why is that?" Maya asked, because she'd made it a rule of thumb that when people weren't happy to see her, that generally meant she was getting closer to something she needed to know.

The guard shrugged, though. "Top floor."

Maya and Marco headed up in an elevator, which was open sided so that Huron seemed to fall away around them, and Lake Erie glittered below in the evening light. When it opened, Maya stepped out, and found herself...

…well, in the last place she expected from some young man who'd been dancing in local competitions a couple of years before. It was lavish on a scale that Maya would never be able to afford unless she won the lottery, with every scrap of furniture looking handmade, and the paintings on the wall looking as if they belonged in a museum or a bank vault rather than an apartment. There was enough computer equipment for a local branch of the FBI set up in one corner, while the whole of one wall was given over to windows with a view out over the lake.

Dane Carlucci was waiting for them. He was around Maya's height, with mid-brown skin, high cheekbones, and a lean dancer's body still. Maya could see the definition of his muscles because he wore workout pants and a tank top. He did *not* look happy to see her and Marco.

"What are you doing here?" he asked. "Tonio is due home soon, and I've had to interrupt my stream to talk to you."

"Your stream?" Maya said.

"I'm a streamer; it's what I do," Dane said. "You know, games, workout videos? I'm an *influencer*."

That caught Maya a little by surprise.

"And you make enough from that to live *here*?" Marco said, articulating it.

"Oh, this is mostly Tonio. He cleaned up on crypto. Now, what do you want? Why are you here, in my home?"

"Anne Postmartin," Maya said, because she wanted to see what kind of a reaction her name would get. Would Dane be afraid that he was about to be caught out? Would he have sympathy for the dead girl?

"That bitch!" Dane said instead, the anger on his face obvious now. "If I'd known you wanted to talk to me about her, I wouldn't have let you up here."

"And why is that?" Maya asked. What was he trying to hide?

"Because she was one of the girls who decided that they were going to make my life hell back at the dance academy," Dane snapped. He still hadn't invited them to come any further into the penthouse. They certainly didn't look like they were going to get close to sitting on any of that handmade furniture. "Do you really think I want to waste any mental energy on thinking back to all that?"

"You don't want to help catch her killer?" Marco asked from the side.

Maya saw Dane shrug. "Catch them, don't catch them. What does it have to do with me?"

"You were at the McFadden Dance Academy at the same time," Maya said. "You were in the same troupe. You knew Anne, and it sounds like you didn't like her. Was it just because Anne was a better dancer than you, Mr. Carlucci?"

It was a confrontational question, but it was pretty obvious that this was destined to be a confrontational interview. At least if Maya asked this kind of question, she might make Dane react enough that he let something slip.

"She wasn't better than me," Dane said. "In practice, I was just as good. Better. Yet somehow, she was the one being picked for all the shows, while the lone little gay boy got ignored. Do you know what it was *like* for me there in the academy?"

"Tell me," Maya said.

She saw Dane look her up and down. "Like you'd get it. Have you ever been anywhere in your life where people didn't treat you like you were some precious flower to be looked after?"

Maya laughed at that, actually laughed, because she couldn't help herself. It was so far off the mark.

"I was the girl who didn't fit in with my class," she said. "The one who joined the military and the FBI. You think I haven't had my share of people looking at me like I don't belong?"

"This was more than looking," Dane said, clearly determined not to let go of whatever moral high ground he'd grabbed. "The girls at that school were total bitches to me. They made me quit."

"How did they do that?" Maya asked.

Dane took on a pained expression, as if just remembering it hurt. "They wouldn't talk to me in the classes. They'd send me these *messages* on social media, just constantly making fun of me. Every time I walked past, it seemed like there would be some little laugh, some joke being made about me."

"You don't look like you've done so badly from it," Marco said.

That was an important consideration. Before she could judge if Dane had been the one to kill Anne, she needed to know just how angry he'd been at being pushed out of the dance studio. Had it really been enough to get him to lure her to a stand of trees and strangle her?

"It worked out well," Dane said. "But that doesn't make it *better*. If you throw me off a cliff and I land in a pile of money, you don't get to claim credit."

"So you were pretty upset at the time?" Maya said. She needed to hear him say it.

"Of course I was," Dane said. "They'd just taken away my dreams. If I'd been like Anne, I would have been a star."

"Is that why you harassed girls there at the studio? Started making threats? You didn't quit, did you Dane? You were asked to leave."

Dane took a step or two back, like he wanted to run off, but where was there to run in the middle of a penthouse?

"It wasn't like that!" Dane insisted. "They were lashing out at me, but when I tried to get back at them, suddenly I'm the bad guy? They spent months harassing me, but now the story's about how I harassed one of them?"

"*One* of them?" Maya said. "Or was that just the start? Were you just building up to something else? When you were thrown out of the studio, did it make you even angrier?"

Dane stared at her for several seconds. Maya could see the small twitches there as he realized just how serious this was. "You think... you think I killed Anne?"

"Did you?" Maya asked.

"No, of course not!" he said. "It wasn't even her I was sending messages to. It was one of the others, Lindsey. Anne wasn't one of the main ones making fun of me. She didn't need to be, when she could just dance and everything would be fine for her."

"And that didn't make you jealous?" Maya asked.

"I wasn't even down at the lake that night," Dane insisted. "I was... I went to this club in Cleveland, got in with a fake ID. Spiders, you know it?"

"I do," Marco said.

Meaning that they had at least a chance of checking Dane's alibi. Not that it was much of one. Finding someone who remembered one underage guy with a fake ID on one specific night two years ago? It was practically impossible to corroborate.

Yet some instinct told Maya that Dane might be telling the truth. When it came to alibis, she'd found that most people didn't have perfect ones, because the only people who cared enough to ensure that they did were the ones who were planning on engaging in something criminal.

Dane had given them something that there *might* be a chance of checking, too, and that wouldn't have been a good move if he was guilty. As much as Maya had hoped that this lead would pan out, he sounded like he was being honest.

Which meant that they had nothing from this.

Maya tried not to let the frustration build inside her, but it was hard, when her deadline was moving forward hour by hour. The time they'd taken to come out to Huron was time they could have used to look at another lead, another piece of evidence.

She tried to salvage something from this, in spite of how badly it had gone.

"Ok, so not you," she said. "What about other people at the studio? Did any of them have a grudge against Anne?"

"Plenty of them were jealous," Dane said. "But I told you, they forced me out. It wasn't like they told me what they were thinking." He paused. "I'd like you to leave now."

And they had no reason to stay. All this way, and they'd gotten no further into the penthouse than a couple of paces, making it easy to back away into the elevator.

"All right," Maya said, as she and Marco prepared to leave. "One last thing. Lucas McFadden, the dance coach. It feels like he's hiding something. Would you know anything about what it is?"

Dane shook his head. "Out of all the dancers there, trust me, *I'm* not the one you need to ask about that."

Maya wanted to ask him what he meant by that, but the elevator doors were already closing, shutting off her chances of finding out more. Maya could feel her mood sinking with the elevator. They'd learned nothing here.

And somewhere, her sister was waiting, kidnapped, with the seconds counting down.

CHAPTER THIRTEEN

Marco tuned the radio of his Explorer to a country music station for the ride back to Cleveland, but more of his attention was on Agent Gray, Maya. He'd found in the last day or so that his attention often strayed her way, but this time, at least, it was purely to do with the case.

"Why ask about the dance coach, when we know it can't be him?" Marco asked, as he guided the Explorer onto the freeway.

"There's still something off about him," Maya said. "He's lying about something, but I don't know what, yet."

She sounded adamant about it, which was strange, given how things had just gone.

"My money's on Carlucci," Marco said. "All that hostility? And he clearly didn't like Anne, however much he tried to make it all about the other girls there. Plus, he was twitchy while we were there."

"He was twitchy *because* we were there," Maya said. "Trust me, when he said he was somewhere else that night, he was telling the truth."

"Why are you so certain?" Marco asked. Maya had been like this almost since she showed up, certain about who was lying and who wasn't, focusing on things Marco wouldn't have considered. On one level, it was a good thing, because it meant that they weren't just going over the same old Moonlight Killer ground, but on another, it was hard to understand.

"I almost went into the Behavioral unit at the FBI," Maya said. "Part of the reason for that was I'd taken all the courses on interrogation and psychology."

"So you looked for his eyes shifting in a particular direction or something?" Marco asked. He hadn't taken any of the courses, but he'd heard the stories passed around the bullpen about the people who had.

"No," Maya said. "But through the conversation I had a baseline of how Dane was reacting. Yes, he was twitchy, but he was *consistently* twitchy. If he'd gone suddenly still and controlled, that would have been more of a tell. And he seemed genuinely upset that we'd think he did it. Not guilty, not afraid, just didn't want his name dragged into it all."

To Marco, all that human lie detector stuff sounded too fanciful to be true. He'd always trusted his gut when it came to that kind of thing, but Maya made it sound like she knew exactly what she was doing.

Marco wasn't sure how far he should trust that. Ordinarily, with a partner, you got years of working together in which to get used to one another. Now, he had to work with someone who had only arrived last night, and who didn't have to listen to him if she didn't want to, because she was FBI.

So far, though, Marco had been impressed by Maya, even if he hadn't always understood what she was doing. She'd found lines of investigation that he hadn't known were there, even if they hadn't panned out yet. More than that, she seemed at least as motivated to solve this as Marco. She didn't feel like some agent wandering in to take a casual look at a cold case in the hope of an easy win for her record.

Yet Marco couldn't shake the feeling that there was more to this. Something Maya wasn't quite telling him. Were there some FBI politics behind the scenes of this? Something that meant that she needed to solve this to keep her career? It would certainly help to explain her motivation.

"What did you make of the last thing Dane said?" Maya asked. "That he wasn't the one to ask about the dance coach?"

"Probably just that he was on the outside at the dance studio, so he can't tell us anything useful," Marco suggested.

"Maybe," Maya said, and Marco saw her bite her lip.

"You don't think so?"

Maya smiled at that. "Ah, now *you're* the expert on body language?"

"Maybe I'm just watching you closely," Marco said. He was, and that was a long way from being a hardship.

"It's just the way that Dane put the emphasis on it, like he couldn't tell us anything, but someone else could."

Marco was pretty sure that he knew what that meant.

"You want to talk to all of the other dancers on the list?"

"Just as many as we need to in order to find out what's going on there," Maya said. "I don't like leaving things like that hanging. What if it's our way into this?"

Marco had to at least allow the possibility, although his doubts about McFadden being the killer remained.

"All right," he said. "But in the morning. There's no way we'll get back before it's dark, and I'm pretty sure the former dancers won't appreciate us just showing up at their doors in the middle of the night."

Maya looked as if she might ask him to do it anyway. Was she really that invested in solving this case? Marco could practically see the conflict running across her face.

"You're sure we can't at least get to some of them now?" Maya asked.

"You're in that much of a hurry?" Marco countered. "I want it solved as much as you do, but this is a cold case, Maya. A marathon, not a sprint."

"I'm not sure I have enough *time* for a marathon," Maya said. "I have to get this finished by the 29th. Midnight."

That caught Marco's attention enough that he almost missed their turn onto the freeway.

"That's a very precise time. And pretty close."

Two more days. Did Maya really think that she could solve a murder in two more days, when no one else had been able to solve this for years?

"What happens then?" Marco asked.

Maya didn't answer.

"Agent Gray, what happens on the 29th?"

"It's just how long I've been given to do this job," she said. "If I can't get it done by then, I'll be pulled out."

Marco shook his head. "Try again."

There was another of those pauses, and Marco pulled over at the side of the freeway.

"You can't pull over here," Maya said.

"If a traffic cop comes to investigate, I'm pretty sure I can talk my way out of it," he replied. "But I'm not moving this car until you tell me what's going on. What happens on the 29th?"

"I'm not sure I can tell you," Maya said. "It's-"

"If you say classified, you're walking back to Cleveland," Marco said. He meant it too. He wouldn't work with a partner who couldn't even trust him that far.

"All right," Maya said, relenting. "But there's only so much I can tell you. We've had a credible threat that's due to be carried out at that time if we don't solve this case."

"What kind of credible threat?" Marco said.

"Someone else will be killed," Maya said. There was a lot of tension in her voice now.

"Who?" Marco asked. He wasn't about to let go of this.

"I don't know, exactly," Maya said. "The threat wasn't specific about that part, but it's something we need to take seriously. I solve this, or someone dies."

"And that's why you're running round trying to cram as much into the day as possible?" Marco said.

"Yes."

Marco had already proven that he was no expert on telling truth from lies, but he had the feeling that this part was true, at least.

"I should tell this to my superiors," he said.

Maya quickly shook her head. "If you do that, all the arguments that follow will kill any chance of getting this done before the deadline. And honestly, does it matter *why* I'm working this case? The fact is that I'm here to try to find Anne's killer, and I'm going to do my level best to find them."

Marco had to admit she had a point there. Maya had made more progress in a couple of days than everyone else, including him, had in two years. He wasn't going to throw that away.

He restarted the car and set off again. "Ok, I can work with that, and with you. But it's still too late to go talking to more dancers. By the time we found them all, it would be the middle of the night. We'll have to start again in the morning."

"All right," she said at last. "I guess I can work the files or something from my hotel room. You'll pick me up early tomorrow?"

"Why not just stay in my spare room, and cut out the drive time?" Marco joked trying to get back some of the light mood that they'd had before. It was only as he said it that he realized how that had to sound. Like he was making a very different kind of offer. "Sorry, I didn't mean-"

"No, it's fine," Maya said quickly. Maybe a shade *too* quickly, or was that just Marco's imagination?

Maybe it was what he was hoping, just as he'd been hoping that Maya would say yes when he jokingly offered her the room. It wasn't that he thought anything could ever happen between them, but a man could hope, couldn't he?

No, he told himself. He had to focus on the job, on catching a killer.

"I'll drop you back at your hotel," Marco said. He turned the radio up slightly, because it was slightly better than trying to make conversation after something like that.

"You really listen to country all the time?" Maya said.

Marco shrugged. "Why not?"

"It's just... you're in Cleveland, not Nashville. Is this some dream of being a small-town sherriff, Marco? Are you just a cowboy at heart?"

Marco laughed at that, feeling some of the tension in the car fade away. Maybe he'd imagined it in the first place. "Nope. I just like the songs."

He could see her watching him.

"No, I'm not sure I believe that," Maya said. "I think I buy the image of you as the loner sheriff far more."

"Is that just the image you want to have of me, Maya?" he shot back. "Me in cowboy boots on horseback? Because honestly, the one time I got on a horse, I fell off."

"Somehow, I doubt that," Maya said. "I'm pretty sure that you'd manage anything physical you put your mind to."

"Thinking of trying to take Lucas McFadden up on those dance lessons?" Marco asked. "Because I think it's a bit late for us to go undercover."

It felt good to be joking around with a partner again. It felt especially good that it was Maya. Marco wasn't going to pretend that he wasn't attracted to her, even if he knew that the odds of anything happening there were pretty low. They were both professionals who needed to focus on their jobs, and in a few days, Maya would probably be gone again.

There was no reason why they couldn't enjoy a little harmless flirting in the meantime though, or how Marco couldn't still find himself wishing that Maya had taken him up on the offer to stay over at his place.

He drove her back to the Best Western she was staying at, pulling up in the parking lot and waiting for her to get out.

"I'll pick you up at eight tomorrow," he said.

"I'll be waiting," Maya promised him.

"Sleep well, Agent Gray."

"You too, Detective Spinelli."

Marco turned to drive off, but his thoughts were still on Maya, and not just in the obvious ways. There was something else to her, something about that level of motivation she had with this case that went beyond even the fact that lives hung in the balance. Marco wanted to know what that was about.

He would pick her up in the morning, sure, but he would also make a few calls first, and try to find out the parts that she wasn't telling him.

CHAPTER FOURTEEN

When she got back to her hotel room, Maya sat there in the dark, just inside the door trying to work out if she'd just made a huge mistake. She'd just told Marco most of the reason for doing this, and if he told his superiors, then what?

Possibly, all kinds of problems. They might try to get rid of her because they didn't like being lied to by the FBI about this being routine. Worse, they might insist on trying to catch the guy who had sent the postcard, and if he really was watching, then that might put her sister in danger.

Just the thought of that made Maya's heart pound with anxiety, so that it took an effort to get up, make it to the light switch, try to behave like everything was ok. Maybe Marco wouldn't say anything.

No, that was too much to hope for.

The only thing to do right now was to try to blank it all from her mind. Maya took a cursory glance round the hotel room, making sure that nothing was out of place, nothing had changed since she left it this morning. After the way the postcard had arrived in her apartment building, Maya wasn't taking any chances.

There was no sign that anyone had been here, though. Everything was as pristine as Maya had left it, the whole room bland and forgettable, with simple, easily replaced décor that was less about being comfortable and more about being repeatable across a huge chain.

Maya knew that she shouldn't have coffee this late, but she drank some anyway, washing it down with bourbon from the minibar. There was no way that she was going to sleep yet, so she got out her laptop, sat on the bed, and started to review those of the files that weren't sitting in a filing cabinet back in the office.

There were too many dead ends. Lucas McFadden had an alibi. Dane Carlucci sounded like he was telling the truth, and in any case, there was no chance of breaking his alibi in the time available. There was no sign of the boyfriend that Maya was so sure Anne had at the time of her death.

She scanned the files, looking for anything else that might help, but the words were starting to swim on the screen by now, either from tiredness, or from drinking the bourbon and coffee too quickly.

All of the dead ends felt like the kind of things that she would have been able to overcome normally. She would have worked through each one slowly, ground down every scrap of evidence no matter how many hours it took. Now, though, every wasted moment was another second closer to the deadline the killer had given her. Another second closer to a woman dying, maybe to Megan dying.

That thought was enough to send Maya's heart pounding again, and she found herself reaching for the bourbon once more. She put it back, though. She couldn't afford to be less than clearheaded tomorrow.

Maya found herself trying to picture where Megan might be, found herself trying to work out how anyone could just kidnap twelve "bunnies" and keep them without anyone noticing. It was never that simple, though.

People went missing all the time, and Maya knew just how many of them were never found. Families assumed that the missing had run off, suffered some kind of breakdown, met someone or gone traveling. They assumed that their loved ones would call, sooner or later. It wasn't like Maya had been good at calling Megan herself.

As for where someone would keep twelve women, people saw what they wanted to see. They would assume a reclusive family, or some kind of retreat, before they thought about people being kept captive. It *might* be possible to track down somewhere like that by looking for unusual transactions, things that had been built that looked unusual, but Maya suspected that she would have to know where to look first, or there was a risk of looking through every warehouse, bunker, outhouse, and illegal pot growing house in the country.

Maya pinched the bridge of her nose, trying to consider the other possibility. What if this was all a hoax? Was it really possible that the maniac who had sent the postcard had her sister? Her only real piece of evidence was one nickname used at the postcard's end, and there were ways someone might have found that out. People could find out anything, these days. Maybe Maya was chasing around, panicking about the deadline, running into dead ends, when none of this was real.

Even if it was, maybe she should be spending her time in a better way, trying to *catch* the guy who was doing this, rather than solving a murder from years ago. Maybe Reyes had been right back in the office, and the only way this ended well was if they managed to track down the guy who'd sent the postcard and went in hard with a tactical team.

A part of Maya wanted to be out there, looking for her sister. She even called up Megan's social media accounts, trying to work out if there was any way to retrace her movements from it. There was nothing there that Maya didn't know already. Practically the first thing she'd done when she'd realized her sister was missing was to go through all this.

Megan's last update had been from San Diego, but Maya had already been there, looking for her, talking to anyone who had been mentioned in a post, anyone her sister might have met.

Maybe she'd even talked to the person who had taken her. Maybe she'd been looking into the eyes of Megan's captor and never known it. At the time, all she'd been thinking was that maybe, if she found the spot Megan had been taken from, there might be some link to where she'd been taken next.

Maya knew it didn't work like that. Whoever had taken her could have moved her anywhere after that. The only real chance was trying to find trace evidence on the postcard, and the others back at headquarters were already doing that. The best thing Maya could do was to keep going, trying to meet the impossible deadline, trying to save a life that way.

When they eventually did find the sick guy who had sent the postcards, though, Maya was going to make sure he paid for it, and if he'd harmed one hair on Megan's head... she'd kill him, FBI or not.

Maya knew that she needed to sleep, so she turned out the light, lay back on the bed, and stared up at the ceiling in the dark. Every noise around her seemed loud now, from cars going past outside to the couple having an argument a few rooms down. It seemed like forever before sleep finally claimed her.

Maya was walking through a maze, the kind made from hedges, where every turning looked the same. She'd been told how you were meant to solve them once, but couldn't remember now, so that the only option was to blunder through it blindly, stopping each time she reached a dead end and trying to retrace her steps.

There was something at the heart of the maze she needed to find; something she needed to get to so desperately that it felt as if she might die if she didn't. Above Maya, a large clock was ticking, counting down the seconds, with every tick feeling like it sliced away a few more of her chances.

There were rabbits bouncing around the maze now, each one small and white, with long floppy ears. They hopped this way and that, and somehow, Maya got it into her head that she needed to follow them. Yet the more she tried to catch up with them, the faster they hopped away from her, so that Maya found herself stumbling into yet more dead ends.

Now, somewhere on the far side of those hedges, Maya could hear Megan's voice.

"Help me, Maya! Please, help me!"

"I can't find the way! Where are you?"

"Help me!"

Maya threw herself at the hedges, clawing at them with her bare hands. They had thorns that tore at her flesh, but she ignored them, digging her way through like she was one of the rabbits there, able to burrow her way through anything. Her arms ran with blood, but Maya ignored it, continuing to move forward.

Now, the hedges seemed to press in on all sides, almost like they'd swallowed her whole. Only they opened out now, forming a kind of tunnel, and the living walls gave way to more ordinary brick, lit by flickering lights ahead and stained with smears that Maya knew to be blood without even checking.

Above, the clock still ticked, down through its last few seconds.

Maya started to run, hurrying along the tunnel, the echo of her footsteps sounding over the tick of the clock. Then there were *only* the footsteps to hear, because above her, the clock fell silent.

"No," Maya said, hearing her own voice echo out. "No!"

She was still running, but everything around her seemed to slow to a crawl. She came out into a large room, with twelve slabs set out there in a circle, like some grim combination of a mortuary and a theater.

Megan lay on all of them. Twelve versions of her, lying there, each one killed in a different way. A part of Maya recognized cases she'd worked on before, images taken from crime scene photos or visits to the mortuary burned into her memory.

On this slab, Megan had been shot a dozen times. On the next, she'd had her throat cut, blood running in a river down the side of the stone. On and on it went, with her sister poisoned, strangled, beaten so badly she wasn't recognizable.

Maya was too late.

"What use is a cold case investigator?" a voice said. "Too late to change anything. Too late to make things better. Too late to save your sister."

"Who are you?" Maya demanded, but she knew it didn't work like that, even in her dream. She turned this way and that, looking for the man who'd spoken.

She turned back, and he was there in front of her, his face shadowed in spite of the lights around, so that she couldn't see who he was, no matter how she twisted and turned to try to find it out.

"There you are," he said. "The last bunny for my collection."

He raised gloved hands, the same as the ones that had been used to strangle Anne Postmartin, and as those hands fastened around her throat, Maya could do nothing to stop them.

Maya woke gasping, her hands scrabbling at her throat where she'd gotten tangled up in the coverlet. She sat up sharply, forcing herself to breathe deeply, while the first of the dawn light spilled in through the window to her hotel room.

"It was just a dream," she said aloud. "It was just a dream."

A dream pulled together from every fear she had about this case. Maya didn't need to be told how easily it could all become a reality. She went through to the bathroom, splashing water on her face and trying to stay calm.

It meant that when her phone went off, she had to run back through into the room, hurriedly searching round for where she'd left it. Maya found it under the bed, and one look at the number told her that she wasn't going to enjoy this.

Deputy Director Harris was calling, and at this time of the morning, that could only mean one thing: trouble.

CHAPTER FIFTEEN

"Sir?" Maya said as she answered Harris's call. She sat on the bed, half imagining that she was in his office. Although she probably wouldn't have been in her pajamas for that.

"Gray, how are things going in Cleveland?" Harris asked, straight to business as usual.

"I'm making progress, following leads," Maya said, because admitting to her boss that she kept running into dead ends didn't seem like the right thing to do.

"What leads?" Harris asked. He clearly wasn't going to let her slide through the conversation without specifics. Maya wouldn't have expected otherwise, but she'd felt like she had to try.

"I'm taking the view that if a whole series of investigators couldn't find the Moonlight Killer, maybe it's worth investigating other options around the killing," Maya said. "It seems like the best chance of getting to the killer before the deadline."

Normally, with cold cases, she was on a long leash. She could go off and investigate with only minimal contact from headquarters. She guessed that the imminent threat to a woman's life changed that.

"And these other options include looking at Anne Postmartin's dance coach?" Harris said. Maya could hear the doubt in his voice.

"At any aspect of her personal life that I can," Maya said. "My working theory is that someone close to her might have killed her, then either they tried to make it look like the Moonlight Killer, or we all just assumed that it was him because of the timing and method of killing."

Maya held her breath. Deputy Director Harris could easily turn around and tell her to focus on the Moonlight Killer. She half expected him to, since catching a notorious serial killer would be a far bigger success than going after some local, and since every other investigation had looked that way.

"All right," Harris said after a second or two. "I buy it, and it makes sense given the short timeframe to look into aspects that haven't been explored. I'm obliged to tell you though that I've had a complaint through from Cleveland's chief of police. Something about you harassing people. There was a young man named Dane Carlucci mentioned, and McFadden, the dance coach you asked for a check on."

A complaint? Maya didn't know what to think about that. Complaints happened, because people didn't like it when she started digging into their lives, but she didn't have time now to start dealing with any fallout from one.

"Carlucci was a former dancer who got in trouble for harassing another dancer at the studio and who was clearly jealous of Anne," Maya explained. "McFadden... well, I went there trying to get more information about Anne, but something was very off about him. Are you telling me to back off?"

"On the dance coach, yes," Harris said. "We ran the check you requested, and his background came back squeaky clean. Those instincts of yours are misfiring this time, Gray."

Maya had a hard time believing that. There was something shifty about the coach, something he was hiding. Yet if his background check was clean and he had an alibi as well, what was she meant to do?

"What about the complaint?" she asked.

"I'm meant to notify you that one has been made," Harris said. "Other than that, I don't see any reason in bothering about it. Some local police chief wants to get apoplectic because the FBI are in town? That's his problem, not yours. Keep digging, and don't pay him any attention."

"Anyone ever tell you you're the best boss?" Maya said.

"Usually right around the time they want a raise," Harris replied, deadpan.

"How are things going over there?" Maya asked.

"We're still looking to see if we can get any leads from the postcard," Harris said. "Plus, I have Reyes and a couple of others trying to track down anything to do with your sister."

"I looked," Maya said. "There isn't anything."

"You know as well as anyone that sometimes, having a fresh pair of eyes on something can help," Harris said. "You keep doing what you're doing. We've got things here."

With that, he hung up, leaving Maya to ponder exactly what they were going to do. Her biggest fear was that they might do something that would put her sister in danger. The kidnapper had been clear about what would happen if they deviated from the rules of his sick game.

A part of her wanted to call Harris back and warn him about the risk to her sister, but even as she reached for her phone, it pinged with a text from Marco.

I'm outside. You said early, right?

Maya had, and it seemed that now he knew the stakes, Marco was just as eager to get going as she was.

Down in five, she texted back, before running to throw on clothes and tie back her hair. She grabbed her things and was out of the door almost at a run. Marco was out in the parking lot, in his usual slightly disheveled ensemble, making it look good as usual. Then Maya looked down and saw what he had on his feet.

"Cowboy boots, really?"

She saw Marco shrug. "I thought I'd try to live up to your expectations, Agent Gray."

He did that, and more, especially when Maya realized something else.

"You didn't tell your bosses about the threat the kidnapper made," Maya said.

"How do you figure that?" Marco said.

"Because I just had a call from *my* boss, telling me that there had been complaints, but there was no mention of that side of things. If you'd told your police chief, he would have used that as an excuse to kick me out."

"He would," Marco agreed, "which is why I couldn't tell him. We need you here, *I* need you here, if we're going to catch Anne's killer."

Maya couldn't believe how much that meant to her. Marco keeping something from his bosses was a big deal. If it got out... well, he could lose his job. Even knowing that, he'd kept his word to her and not said anything.

"I guess your boss wasn't happy about the complaints?" Maya said.

Marco nodded, and led the way round to the Explorer, getting in.

"He spent a good five minutes yelling at me for not keeping you under control," Marco said, as Maya took her own side of the car. She was starting to think of it as hers now, even though she would be there, at most, another couple of days. "His precise words were 'you're there as her handler, so handle her.'"

"Not a man to notice a double entendre then?" Maya said.

Marco let out a short laugh at that. "I think he was too pissed at you to notice much of anything."

"Sorry to cause you that much trouble," Maya said, and she found that she *was* sorry. She didn't want to end this leaving Marco to deal with all the fallout. At the same time, though, she would do whatever she needed to do in order to solve this case and save her sister.

"I'm used to trouble," Marco said. "But the chief specifically warned us off Lucas McFadden and Dane Carlucci."

"Who would have thought that dancers had so many connections?" Maya said.

Marco leaned over to take a box from the glove compartment. Maya wasn't entirely surprised when it contained doughnuts.

"You're just determined to live up to every 'local cop' stereotype, aren't you?" Maya said.

"Only the ones you find endearing. And the tasty ones, of course" Marco offered her a doughnut and Maya took it, telling herself that it was only because there hadn't been any time for breakfast.

"There," Marco said. "We'll have you two hundred pounds and riding out the time to your retirement in no time."

Maya felt a little guilty at that comment because it was too close to the kind of thing she'd expected from Marco before she'd actually met him. Still, she bit into the doughnut gratefully, and it was exactly the right combination of unhealthy ingredients to feel good.

"You keep providing good doughnuts, and you might just get me to stick around forever," Maya said.

"Then I'll have to get more."

Maya found that the banter with the detective was exactly what she needed to drive away the last memories of last night's bad dreams. Focusing on Marco meant that for at least a moment or two, Maya wasn't consumed by the thought that her sister might already be dead.

"So, where are we going today if we're meant to keep away from the dance studio?" Marco asked.

Maya thought about that, trying to think of somewhere that wasn't linked to Lucas McFadden. The problem was that trying to avoid him only brought more thoughts of him. In spite of Harris' warnings, she couldn't shake the feeling that there was something wrong there. She wanted to keep digging into the dance studio.

"We were told to keep away from the dance instructor," Maya said. "Nobody said anything about ignoring everyone connected to the dance studio. The other dancers in McFadden's little troupe can still tell us more about Anne, and what was happening the night she was killed.

They would have been at the show, so maybe one of them saw something they're only remembering now."

"You're just hoping they give you more on their coach," Marco said.

Maya shook her head, though. "Not just that. I don't have time to waste. If I thought that there was a better lead out there, we'd be going after it."

Today and tomorrow was all they had left. They couldn't afford to waste a moment of it, but this didn't feel like a waste to Maya. There was something that she was missing about Anne's life, something that the other dancers around her might be able to give her.

She took out the list that Petronella had given them before. Lucy Adams was the first name.

"I guess we start at the top of the list and work our way down," Maya said. "Do you think you can find an address for Lucy Adams without it being a problem down at your precinct?"

"That's just records," Marco said. "It shouldn't be a problem. We're doing the whole list?"

"As many as we need to," Maya said.

Marco made a call. "Hey Ed, I have a list of names I need addresses for. Yeah, I'll photograph it and send it through to you."

He did exactly that, which left Maya and him sitting there, with nothing to do but wait, and waiting was painful now, because Maya could feel the time dripping away, little by little.

"We'll catch whoever did this in time," Marco assured her, and just the fact that he'd guessed what was on Maya's mind was impressive. It was also a little worrying. Had she really let someone get so close that he could read her like that?

Maya didn't like having people that close. If all of this with Megan had proved anything, it was just how easily that could get them hurt. That wasn't going to be a problem, though. She reminded herself that in a couple of days, whether she succeeded or failed, she was going to be leaving, and probably wouldn't see Marco again.

So why did she feel a twinge of disappointment at that?

Before she could examine that thought, she heard Marco's phone buzz with a message.

"Got the addresses," Marco said, and started the engine of the Explorer. "Lucy Adams, right?"

Maya nodded. "We'll start at the top and work down."

She had to hope that this was the right choice. That they would get something that might lead them to the killer. If not, then they were wasting time that they didn't have.

CHAPTER SIXTEEN

Lucy Adams lived in an apartment with a couple of friends, who hovered around so much that Maya thought about asking them to leave the cramped confines of the living room, simply so that it wouldn't interfere with the interview.

She knew that she couldn't do that, though, because it would only make getting Lucy to talk to her harder. Currently, the young woman was sitting on a sofa that seemed far too large for just her, wearing workout clothes like she was about to go for a run and huddled up as if to keep Maya and Marco out. She was blonde haired and skinny in a way that looked unhealthy to Maya and made her want to make the girl something to eat.

She was clearly getting old, turning into her mother.

"We just want to ask you a couple of questions about Anne, Lucy," Maya said. "How well would you say you knew her?"

"Pretty well, I guess," Lucy said. "I mean, we were both members of the main troupe, back at the dance school, not just walk ins."

"What do you mean by walk ins?" Maya asked. She kept the questions light for now, wanting to try to get the girl to feel at ease.

"People who just come in for a few classes, but they never really make it to the troupe," Lucy said. "They aren't *serious*."

"And you were serious," Maya said. It wasn't even a question. "Like Anne?"

She saw Lucy nod. "She was going to be a star."

That seemed to be what everyone around Anne thought. Maya found herself wondering if it would have played out that way for her. For every person who actually found fame, there had to be a hundred more where everyone around them thought they had all the talent in the world. Still, if she was within a shot of winning the nationals, Anne must have been pretty good.

"You sound very certain," Maya said.

"It wasn't just that she was pretty, or that she could dance," Lucy said. "We could all *dance*. It was more... when she walked into a room, it was like the rest of the room stopped. She was the standard that we all had to try to live up to."

96

"It must have been tough, trying to do that," Maya said. "What was it like, in the dance studio?"

Maya caught the pause before Lucy answered. Her expression became happy and bright, but in a fixed kind of way, like she'd practiced it for exactly this kind of moment.

"Everything was fine."

"So you didn't spot any problems there?" Maya asked. "There wasn't any kind with Lucas McFadden and Anne?"

"No, no, of course not," Lucy said, with that same too tight expression. There was a finality to her tone that said she wasn't going to talk any more about that.

"What about the night of the show?" Maya asked. "Did Anne seem different in any way?"

"I don't know," Lucy said. "Maybe… like distracted, but she'd been distracted for a few weeks. If it had been anyone else, they'd have been in trouble for slacking so close to a big show."

"Did you resent the fact that she wasn't in trouble?" Marco asked, from the side.

"No, of course I didn't," Lucy said. "Anne was my friend."

"Of course," Maya said. "And you were with the other members of the troupe all through the show, right? And afterwards?"

Lucy nodded. That fit with the witness statements at the time. Everyone had been together. No one had seen the moment Anne had left.

"Did anyone slip away from the group?" Maya asked. "Even for a little while?"

"Not alone," Lucy said. "A couple of people went off in pairs to go get changed and get food and things. But with it being down by the lake, no one wanted to be alone."

And yet Anne had deliberately gone off alone to meet whoever had killed her. That was the part Maya couldn't understand, and that kept bringing her back around to the same theory.

"Do you know who Anne's boyfriend was, Lucy?" she asked. Better to ask who he was, rather than if she had one, because people tended to offer more information when they thought you already knew something.

Lucy frowned at that. "I don't know. I don't even think she had a boyfriend right then. There was nothing on her Insta about one."

It was the same answer that she'd had from Anne's other friends.

"Was there anyone behaving suspiciously around the performance?" Marco asked. "Anything there that stood out as unusual?"

"Aside from Anne not being there for the afterparty?" Lucy said. She shook her head. "No."

"If you think of anything," Maya said, taking out a card. "Or if you want to talk about anything else, call me."

They went outside, back to the Explorer, and Maya tried to hold in her frustration at getting answers that she'd already heard. She needed something new, something that would point them in the right direction.

"She was lying about things being fine in the dance studio, wasn't she?" Marco said.

Maya nodded. "You caught that?"

"I paid attention when you were talking about lies last night," Marco said. "She was so closed off for most of it, but for that one thing, her whole body language changed."

"Like she'd practiced making it look normal when she said things were fine so much that she couldn't stop herself," Maya said.

"So what do we do about it?" Marco replied.

There was only one thing they could do, when they couldn't just go back to the studio and drag answers out of Lucas McFadden.

"We need to talk to more dancers," Maya said.

*

Charisma Evans lived in her parents' house, which was exactly as suburban and white picket fence as Anne's had been. The only real difference was that, where all Anne's dance mementos had been crammed into one cabinet, Charisma's were spread all over the house. Just walking in, Maya spotted a big picture of her smiling with the other members of the dance troupe, with Lucas McFadden standing at the heart of them, one arm around Anne's shoulders.

"Can I get you anything to eat or drink?" Charisma's mother asked, bustling through towards a large, open kitchen. "Iced tea, perhaps?"

"Thank you, but no," Maya said with a smile. "We won't take up that much of your time. We just need to talk to Charisma."

She was sitting in the living room, reading a book that she only put down when she'd carefully marked the place. She was almost as tall as Maya was, with tan skin, relatively broad shoulders, and close-cropped hair. She was dressed in a shapeless hooded top and jeans and sitting on a rocking chair.

"You want to ask me all about Anne's death, right?" she said.

"And about her life, too," Maya replied. There was a small sofa off to one side. She took one side of it and Marco got the other. Maya did her best to ignore the weight of his presence next to her, although it was hard to, with him that close. "Tell me about her. Who were her friends? Did she have a boyfriend?"

"I don't know," Charisma said. "We didn't really talk outside the troupe, and when we were there, it was all about getting better. I don't *think* she had a boyfriend when she... when the show happened, but I could be wrong."

"And everyone at the show stayed together pretty much all evening?" Maya asked.

"Yes. I went over this with the police at the time," Charisma said.

"I know. I just want to make sure that I have it all right," Maya said. She also wanted to give the young woman a chance to remember anything she'd forgotten. "No one slipped away? No one was out of sight of anyone else?"

"I don't think so," Charisma said.

Honestly, was there any chance that people would remember this far back? They'd told themselves the story of everyone being there so much that even if someone had slipped out, they would probably all be convinced it hadn't happened. Working with cold cases, Maya knew how locked into the stories they'd told people became over time, so that they actually remembered the story more than what had happened.

"What was the atmosphere like in the dance troupe at the time?" Maya asked.

She could see all the signs of nervousness in Charisma as she answered: shifting in her seat, hands knotting together so that they wouldn't move too much, not looking at her when she'd been looking before.

"Everything was fine," she said.

"Are you sure about that, Charisma?" Maya asked. "Whatever was happening, we can try to help."

"It was fine," the former dancer repeated, and it seemed clear to Maya that she wasn't going to get any more out of her on that topic.

"What about your dance coach?" Maya asked. "What was he like?"

"He was fine," Charisma said, again without any life to the words, or sense that she was going to say more than that.

99

Maya was getting tired of dead ends, especially when it seemed clear that there was something that Charisma wasn't saying, just as there had been something that Lucy Adams wouldn't say. What was going on in that dance studio? The more Maya asked that question, the more she was convinced that, whatever it was, it had something to do with Anne's death.

She went through the routine of taking out a card and setting it down next to Charisma as she stood up. It was obvious that they weren't going to get anything else here.

"Listen," she said. "I can't make you answer any questions. You're not a suspect in any of this, and you're not in any kind of trouble, but it's obvious that there's more going on here. If you want to talk about it, just call me, ok. Please. The only way things get better is if we find out the truth."

Charisma shook her head. "Things don't get better. Do you know what it's like losing someone you were next to every day? Who was there one day and gone the next? And then you can never get away from that, because even years later, people come back asking questions about it all?"

Maya understood all of that, and not just because she'd seen it on other cold cases. When she'd realized that her sister had gone missing, it had been like nothing else in the world made sense anymore.

"I'm sorry that we bothered you," Maya said, going to leave. Mrs. Evans went to show them out.

"Charisma doesn't smile anymore," she said, pausing in the hall, in front of the photograph of the troupe. "She used to be so happy, see? But now she doesn't smile."

Maya obliged her by looking at the photograph again, at the spot where Charisma was smiling for the camera. All the others showed a dozen girls and Dane Carlucci all there in their dance outfits.

Wait... a dozen? No, it wasn't a dozen. Maya counted them, one by one. Then she took the list of names out of her pocket and counted those. She counted them both again, wanting to be sure.

There were fourteen girls in the photograph, but only twelve names on the list. Even allowing for Anne, that left one unaccounted for.

Reaching out, Maya snatched the picture down from the wall.

"What are you doing?" Mrs. Evans asked.

Maya was already hurrying back through to the living room, putting the picture down in front of Charisma.

100

"Charisma, can you tell me the names of all the girls in this photograph?" she said.

"What? Why?"

"Please, it might be important."

"Well, that's me, obviously, and that's Anne. That's…"

Charisma kept naming the girls there, and with each one, Maya checked the name off against her list. Finally, only one girl hadn't been named. Maya pointed to her.

"And her? Who is that?"

"That's Connie, Connie… Ibbotson, Petronella's niece. You know, the receptionist from the dance studio?"

Maya knew, and she knew something else: Petronella, with her "good memory," had left her own niece's name off the list. Maya wanted to know the reason why.

CHAPTER SEVENTEEN

As they headed over to Connie Ibbotson's home, Maya couldn't help feeling that they might finally have caught a break in this case. Why would Petronella leave her niece's name off the list if she wasn't worried about what Maya and Marco would find out when they questioned her?

First, they had to find her. They pulled up outside her apartment building, but there was no one home, no answer when they knocked on the door. Maya cursed in frustration, then turned to see an older woman looking out at her from another apartment.

"We're looking for Connie," Maya said. "Do you know when she'll be home?"

"Not until she's done with work. She works over at Mo's, on the corner."

"Thank you," Maya said, and they headed down, looking around for somewhere that looked likely. On another day, she might have left this and come back when Connie was home, but today, there was no time. They needed to break this case open, and they needed to do it now.

"There," Marco said, pointing to a coffee shop that declared itself to be *Mo's*.

The two of them headed over, and one good thing about having looked at the photograph in Charisma's house was that it made identifying Connie easy. She moved between tables, wearing slacks and a t shirt with a silhouette of a ballet dancer on it. She was of middle height, slender and toned, tanned and with her dark hair tied back away from her face.

"Connie?" Maya said, approaching.

"I'm sorry, do I know you?"

Maya flashed her badge as discretely as she could. "Can we talk? It's about Anne Postmartin's death."

She saw Connie freeze at that, but that didn't necessarily mean anything, just that she was taking a moment to process the sudden arrival of the FBI in her workplace.

"Mo, I need to take my break," she called over to a large, middle-aged barista leaning on the counter.

"You've another hour before that," he called back.

Maya flashed her badge in his direction. "She needs to take her break."

They sat down at one of the tables, with Connie pushing the chair out as far as she could from it without bumping into another customer. Was she poised to run? Marco seemed to think so, because he was poised on the edge of his seat like a sprinter ready to leap out of the blocks.

"Did you have to do that?" Connie asked. "It's hard finding a job that will fit in around dancing gigs, and I can't afford to get fired."

"You're still dancing?" Maya asked, and it took her a moment to realize why she was surprised. Looking at the others they'd spoken to so far, there had been no real indication that they'd still been dancing. Dane Carlucci had given it up completely.

"I get gigs now and then," Connie said. "I know most of the others gave up, but I still want to keep going." She managed a smile. "Still waiting for that big break, you know?"

Washington wasn't LA, where they said every waiter had a script ready to show a producer, but Maya knew how it went. People clinging onto their dreams, hoping that for *them* it would work out.

"Why *have* so many of the others stopped dancing?" Maya asked.

Connie went quiet for a moment or two, looking away. "You'd have to ask them that. Anne's death, I guess. Or just realizing how hard it can be."

Both of those sounded like reasonable explanations, but from the way Connie was suddenly closing off her body language, folding her arms defensively, Maya wasn't sure that she believed either one.

"Ok," she said. "Then I'll ask you a different question: why did your aunt leave you off a list she gave us of dancers in the troupe who might have known Anne?"

That seemed to take Connie by surprise. "She did that?"

"She did that," Marco confirmed, leaning in from the side. It wasn't good cop bad cop, exactly, but it was close. "And the only reason we can think of why she might have is if she thought there was something incriminating we would find if we looked too close at you."

"I mean, maybe it was just because I'm family?" Connie said.

Maya shook her head. "If it were just that, she would have put you on as the first name, so it's clear you're innocent. What was she trying to hide from us? What are we going to find when we look deeper at you?"

"Nothing!" Connie insisted. "Ok, maybe something. Maybe you'll hear that Anne and I were these big rivals. She was always the number one dancer, and I... well I was always number two. I tried so hard to be the best, and she was always just this little bit better."

That sounded a lot like the kind of motive Maya had hoped to find when she started looking at the other dancers in the school. She looked Connie over, trying to gauge if she might have had the strength to strangle Anne to death, or the ruthlessness to do it just to take her top spot.

"I know how that sounds," Connie said. "I know what you're thinking."

"Rivalry can be a pretty powerful motive," Maya said, trying to put it as neutrally as she could. "Eventually, you can get sick of being in someone's shadow."

"I wanted to succeed," Connie said, "but I would never have done anything to hurt Anne."

"You said that she was always a little bit better. She got all the best roles. She was the one who was going to be a star, just like you wanted. Just like you *want*."

"And seeing her there like that made me want to push to do *better*," Connie insisted. "Every time Anne got to be the star, I knew I had to work harder. If she hadn't been there, I wouldn't have been half the dancer I was."

"But you would have gotten her roles," Marco said. Obviously he wasn't any more willing to let this go than Maya was.

"What roles?" Connie asked. "A few spots in local shows? Maybe if I could have made the nationals, but that wouldn't have happened for me even without Anne there. It *didn't* happen for me, you can check. I dance shitty gigs in minor shows, and have slimy guys trying to push me to dance in their strip clubs. You think I would kill my friend for that?"

"So you're saying that you and Anne were on good terms?" Maya asked.

"On good terms?" Connie said. "Anne was my *friend*. Here..."

She reached into her pocket and pulled out a phone. She flicked through, then held it out for Maya to see. There was photograph after photograph of Connie and Anne at dance contests and shows, hugging. There were a couple of them hanging out at parties, obviously friends.

"Go through my social media," Connie said. "You won't see a single negative comment between me and Anne. She was the best, sure, but she pulled me along like a beacon. She got roles, and I'd get somewhere in the cast because people would ask her who the best dancers were. I could have followed her all the way to the top, but instead, I'm working here and dancing places I wouldn't have touched two years ago. I didn't kill Anne."

Maya felt the frustration of running into another dead end, because she believed Connie. It was obvious that the young woman had been Anne's friend, and that she hadn't gained anything from Anne's death. She simply didn't have a good motive to kill her, even before they started to get into the question of if she could have done it. If she'd hated Anne with a vengeance, maybe Maya would have looked for some way around the issue of whether she could have so easily strangled Anne, and then dragged her body down to the shore.

"Ok," Maya said. "I believe you."

"Then can I get back to my work?" Connie asked.

"One thing first," Maya said. "What was going on at the dance studio?"

Maya caught Connie's response: another look away, a shift in her chair like she wanted to run.

"Nothing," Connie said, and there was a difference in her voice too, so that it was flatter, less impassioned.

"A lot of people have been saying that," Maya said, looking at her carefully. "I didn't believe them, either. Your aunt wanted you kept out of this. If it wasn't because you were the killer, my guess is that there was something going on at the dance studio, and she wanted your name kept out of it. Something that got her fired. Something that no one wants to talk about."

"You're imagining things," Connie said, and stood up. "I have to get back to work. My break's over."

It seemed obvious that she wasn't going to answer any more questions, and Maya didn't have a good way to force her to. Maybe she could use the fact that her aunt had lied as leverage, but that kind of thing was never a good way to secure real cooperation. It was the kind of thing best saved for unpicking organized crime, not cold cases.

Maya let her go, looking across the table to Marco. "I'm not wrong, am I? There's *something* going on around that dance studio that they don't want us to know."

"They all react the same way when you talk about it too," Marco said. "Like they've been coached to say nothing."

Coached. Maya was sure that their dance coach was at the heart of this now, but she'd been specifically warned off him. It felt like having to conduct her investigation with one hand tied behind her back. It meant that now, instead of pushing for answers, she and Marco had to simply get up and leave the café.

As they did so though, a figure came stalking towards them. Maya reacted on instinct, reaching towards her gun, but a second later she realized that it wasn't that kind of threat. It was Lucas McFadden, looking red faced with anger.

"What are you doing here?" he demanded.

"I could ask you the same question, Mr. McFadden," Maya said. "What are you doing, and how did you find us?"

"Do you think people don't tell me things?" McFadden said. "I know everyone in this town. I know all the people who matter. Of course someone's going to tell me when you start going around my students, asking questions about me. You were told to back off."

"I was *asked* to keep away from you and your studio," Maya said. "But the dancers in your troupe knew Anne Postmartin, and it's only right that I ask them what they know about the circumstances of her death."

"And about me?" McFadden demanded.

"What are you so afraid of us finding out, Mr. McFadden?" Maya asked. "Why don't you want us talking to the dancers you used to train? Why don't you train them anymore?"

"There you go again, with questions that don't have anything to do with all this," McFadden said. "I tried nicely to get you to back off."

"Making a complaint is *nice*?" Marco asked, stepping up to Maya's side.

"I tried things the nice way," McFadden said. "But you obviously aren't getting the message. Back off, now, or you'll regret it."

"Are you threatening a federal agent, Mr. McFadden?" Maya asked.

"Just back off!" McFadden said, turning to walk away. "I know people. If you don't stop poking your nose in where it's not wanted, I'll have your jobs, both of you!"

It wasn't the first time Maya had been threatened, and this threat only made her more determined. If Lucas McFadden wanted her away from the case that badly, it told her one thing: she was looking in the right direction.

106

There was no way she was going to stop digging into the dance studio now.

CHAPTER EIGHTEEN

Maya was still seething from the arrival of Lucas McFadden as she and Marco made their way back to the car.

"Where to?" he asked. "Are we still making our way down the list?"

It was a valid question, both because they'd hit so many dead ends already with it, and because of the threats McFadden had just made. If he really did know the people who mattered in Cleveland, this could cost them big.

At least, it could cost Marco. Maya was FBI, so she was pretty sure that the local authorities wouldn't be a problem for her. They *could* be a problem for Marco though. Did Maya really want to damage his career for this?

The answer to that should have been obvious. Her sister's life was at stake, so she would do whatever it took, even if that meant that some local cop got in trouble, got suspended, lost his job. None of that should have mattered next to Megan's safety.

The problem was that Maya *liked* Marco. He seemed like a genuinely good person, and a good cop to boot. More than that, Maya had been able to feel the chemistry between them pretty much from the moment they'd met. If she'd run into him in a bar rather than on a case, there would have been no question about where things were going between them.

All those reasons meant that she felt as if she had to at least ask his opinion.

"What do you think we should do?" Maya asked. "Do you want to back down now?"

"Because some guy is making vague threats?" Marco said. He shook his head. "You've told me what the stakes are. I'm not giving up that easily, and I think you're right about there being something wrong at the dance studio. Maybe something happened there, and that's why Anne was missing practices. Maybe that's what got her killed."

"The only way to find that out is to keep going down the list," Maya said. "Assuming any of them tell us anything."

That was the frustrating part of all this. She was pretty sure that, whatever the big secret was, it was the key to this case. She was also pretty sure that talking would only cause trouble for Lucas McFadden. Yet none of his former dancers were prepared to talk about it, or about him. How much of a grip did he have over them? How much of a grip *could* one dance coach have over a town?

"One of them will say something," Marco said. "We'll find *one* who isn't afraid to talk, and then the rest will come rushing."

Maya had to hope that it would be as simple as that, yet she had to remind herself that it often did work that way when it came to cold cases. There was a lot of going over old ground, a lot of frustration, but one piece of evidence could make things fall together quickly. She had to trust that it would be like that in this case.

Maya was still trying to convince herself of that when her phone started to ring. Taking it out, she saw Deputy Director Harris's name, and braced herself for another conversation about not harassing dance coaches. Had Lucas McFadden really worked that quickly?

"Sir?" she said, answering.

"Gray, we have a breakthrough on the case," Harris was usually good at keeping his voice professional, but even so, Maya could hear the excitement in his voice.

"A breakthrough? You know who killed Anne Postmartin?"

"What? No," Harris said. "I meant the *kidnappings*."

Of course he did. Maya had been so focused on the killing in Cleveland that she hadn't even been thinking about the FBI's continued efforts to find the kidnapper. She'd assumed that it would be more or less impossible, unless the kidnapper was very careless. A man who could successfully kidnap twelve women wouldn't be careless.

"What's the breakthrough?" Maya asked.

"Reyes succeeded in tracing the postcard back to where it was sent from," Harris said. "He says it was rerouted through a dummy address, but he managed to crack it. We have an address in Pittsburg. An old apartment building 214 Breyer Street."

Could it be that simple, Maya wondered? Could the kidnapper really be keeping a dozen women in a rundown apartment building in Pittsburg? Or were they working a hoax from there, staying close so that they could see if Maya bit on the bait they dangled? Was it someone sitting alone in an apartment complex, feeling very superior because they'd managed to trick the whole FBI into dancing to their tune?

109

"Reyes really managed to find an address from the postcard?" Maya said, not quite able to believe it. The only name and address on it had been the one pointing to Anne Postmartin. For Reyes to find another from it said either that the kidnapper had made a big mistake, or something was wrong.

"This doesn't sound right, sir," Maya said. "How was it so easy to find the address?"

"It's only easy because we're good at our jobs, Gray," Harris said. "We're gathering a tactical team together in the Pittsburg office to raid the building now."

"A tactical team?" Maya said. "But what about the threat the sender made to kill the hostages if he saw any sign that we were hunting for him?"

Terror for her sister flooded through Maya then. Were her colleagues about to get Megan killed? Were they about to charge in blindly and risk everything?

"Then we make sure that he *doesn't* see us, not until we go in there and arrest him," Harris said.

"Sir, please," Maya said. "Don't be hasty. I'm making progress on the case at this end."

She couldn't see Harris' look of disapproval, but Maya could guess it was there.

"What's the first rule of the playbook when it comes to hostage situations?" Harris said.

"You don't just give the hostage takers what they want, because it doesn't guarantee that the hostages will be safe," Maya said.

"And because they learn that they can get what they want by taking hostages," Harris added. "You solve this case for the kidnapper, you really think they're going to let anyone go?"

"I think it's our best shot," Maya said. She had to believe it. She had to hope that if she solved this case, then her sister would be safe.

Across from her, she could see Marco looking on with a worried expression. He couldn't hear Harris' side of the conversation, but it had to be pretty clear from Maya's half what was going on.

"Well, I think that our best shot is to catch this guy and free every hostage," Harris said. "So that's what we're going to do."

"Sir-" Maya began, determined to argue her case.

"No, Gray, it's happening. We're already getting the tactical team together. The raid is going to happen within the next hour."

"This could be a trap," Maya insisted. "It could be set up deliberately to lure us away if we come looking."

"After all the work it took to find it?" Harris countered. "If he wanted to trap us, he would have left the address of this place on the postcard. Sometimes, we just get a break."

"And sometimes, that's what they want you to think," Maya said.

She knew she wasn't making any headway, though. Harris sounded determined.

"You're too close to this, Gray," Harris said. "You're being cautious because you're worried about your sister, and I get that, but I have to make the calls that stand the best chance of catching this bastard. The tactical team *is* going in."

"At least wait for me to get there," Maya said. "I want to be a part of this. I might be able to spot something that helps while we're there."

"I know you're a one-woman wrecking crew, Gray," Harris said. "But I think a whole tactical team should be enough to take care of one bad guy. We have a location; we have hostages in danger. I don't see any reason to wait. I'll let you know when we have this guy in custody and your sister is safe. Assuming he even has her."

"Sir-" Maya began again, but Harris chose that moment to hang up.

Maya punched the top of Marco's Explorer in frustration.

"Hey!" Marco said. "What's so bad that you're putting dents in my car?"

"*More* dents," Maya corrected him. "And the people back at head office are being idiots. They're so certain that they've found the kidnapper that they're charging forward with a tactical team, trying to save the day."

"It could work out," Marco said.

"It could also mean walking straight into a trap. I need to be there."

"Where?" Marco asked.

"Pittsburg."

"That's a two-hour drive," he pointed out.

Maya knew that, but right then, it didn't matter. Reason didn't come into it. Time didn't come into it. If there was any chance that her sister was in that building, then Maya had to get there.

"I'll drive you," Marco said.

"I can get a car," Maya insisted. "I can hire one, or get one from your precinct's pool, or-"

"Not in time," Marco pointed out. "So I'll drive you."

Even then, it was going to be tight. They leapt into the beat-up old Explorer, and Marco got out a magnetic light to stick on the roof.

"How fast will this thing actually go?" Maya asked.

"Don't knock Betsy here. She's faster than she looks."

"You named your car?" In another moment, Maya might have made fun of Marco for that, but now, the urgency of the situation drove all thoughts of that from her mind. "You know what, so long as you can get us there, I don't care."

"I can get us there," Marco said, and pulled off at a speed Maya normally associated with Hollywood chase scenes.

She'd done driving courses in the FBI, because there was always a chance that she would have to chase down a criminal in a car, but she'd never actually had to do it. It meant that she was left clinging to her seat while Marco wove through traffic at speed, lights flashing and siren blaring.

Once they got out onto the freeway, he only accelerated.

"I may have made one or two modifications to Betsy over the years," Marco said, as they shot out past a truck, leaving it behind.

Maya dared a glance at the speedometer, saw it was well over a hundred, and stopped looking.

There was something terrifying about being in a car with someone driving as fast as they could. Maya didn't mind dangerous situations, she was driving straight towards one, but she usually preferred being the one in control.

Right now, though, she just had to trust that Marco knew what he was doing, even though the traffic was flashing past so quickly that Maya could barely keep up with it.

"Get out of the way, idiot!" Marco yelled, hitting his horn in addition to the siren. Maya felt the car swerve as they overtook on the inside, not slowing down even for a moment. Rain started to pour down outside, but they didn't slow down for that either. Maya didn't want to think about what would happen if they skidded on the slick road surface.

She found that she trusted Marco though. If anyone was going to drive her along at this kind of speed, she was glad that it was him. She felt as safe there in his car as if she'd been held in his arms.

The miles sped by, faster than Maya would have guessed was possible. Even so, it seemed to take forever, simply because of the distances involved. As much as Maya willed the gap between her and her sister to shorten faster, there was only so fast even Marco could drive.

Finally though, Maya caught sight of it there in the distance, with the first signs of industrial buildings and houses out on the outskirts. They were approaching Pittsburg.

Now Maya just had to hope that they were in time.

CHAPTER NINETEEN

Maya clung on as they raced through Pittsburg at a speed that felt anything but safe. Traffic got out of their way as Marco followed the route on his GPS towards Breyer Street, but they skimmed close enough to some of it that Maya was worried that they might scrape along the side of a car at any moment.

As they got closer, Marco killed his lights and sirens. It was the right thing to do to avoid alerting the kidnapper if the raid was still building up, but it also meant that they had to slow down, moving through traffic at a slower pace. With every moment that followed, Maya found herself hoping that they would be in time, felt her excitement building with the prospect of the raid to come.

As soon as they turned the corner of Breyer Street, all of that slipped away from her, leaving an empty feeling inside.

There were police cars parked openly in front of a derelict apartment building that had to be their target. A swarm of uniformed people stood outside, with local cops, paramedics, and a few in tactical gear who looked like they were from a local SWAT team. There were a couple of tactical vans, and at least three ambulances there. Even as she watched, Maya saw one move off, lights flashing.

They'd missed the raid.

That much was obvious from the fact that everyone was out there in the open. If this had been the build up to the raid, the police cars would have been parked in side streets and the vans would have pulled up quietly. The aim would have been not to alert anyone inside. Only now that the raid was done with could the whole circus come out into the open.

"It might still have been a success," Marco said, obviously guessing at her disappointment. "Those might be the hostages they're taking away in the ambulances."

Maya nodded, but as they drove closer, she could see more of people's faces. This didn't *look* like a successful raid.

There was a police cordon near the building, apparently to keep back a cluster of reporters and camera crews who had gathered to cover what was happening. Maya and Marco pulled up next to it, and a uniformed officer moved into their path as they approached.

"Gray, FBI," she said, showing her badge. "This is Detective Spinelli. He's with me. What happened here?"

"If you want details, you'll need to talk to the people in charge," the cop said, waving her to where a trio of figures seemed to be in the middle of an argument. "Good luck."

Maya slipped past the cordon and headed in the direction of the three figures there. One wore an FBI tactical vest, another was in full SWAT gear, and a third appeared to be a lieutenant of the Pittsburg PD. As she and Marco got closer, she made out more details of their argument.

"...telling you that it wasn't my call," the FBI agent said. "My office just got a call from headquarters, asking us to organize the raid because they had the location for a multi-state kidnapper. I was acting on intelligence."

"FBI intelligence is starting to look more and more like a contradiction in terms," the local lieutenant said. He gestured to the cameras. "Do you have any idea how this is going to make us look?"

"Do you think I care how this looks right now?" the SWAT officer asked. "Three of my people were hurt."

Maya realized that if she waited, the three of them would probably argue it back and forth all day, and she didn't have the patience for that right then.

"Agent Gray, FBI," she said, approaching. "What happened here? Did you recover any of the hostages?"

"*Hostages*?" the SWAT officer said. "No, we didn't recover any hostages."

"Gray?" The FBI agent said. "Is this your shit-show?"

"I was arguing *against* this," Maya said. "I'm covering a different angle of the same case, but I need to know what's going on."

"What's going on is that we've put resources and effort in for nothing," the FBI agent said.

"Your office has made us look stupid," the lieutenant agreed. "Sending us off on a raid on an empty house."

"Empty?" That word only made Maya feel worse, because it told her just how badly the FBI had been tricked. Harris and the others had thought they'd outsmarted the kidnapper, but if this was an empty house... they'd played right into his hands. They'd shown that they were hunting for him.

115

They'd shown that they were breaking the rules of his game.

"See for yourself," the SWAT officer said, gesturing to the apartment block. "But be careful. A booby trap has already put three of my guys in the hospital, and for what?"

Maya stared up at the apartment block. Most of the windows were boarded up. There was graffiti at ground level around most of it, and the few windows that weren't covered by boards were broken. She started towards it almost without thinking, Marco following in her wake.

Maya stopped at the doors, which had been blown off their hinges as the team gained entry. She could imagine them now, stacking up behind the leader, the first one blowing the doors, the second going in with a shield, the rest following quickly behind, making sure they didn't cross one another's lines of fire.

"They went in fast," Maya said. She stepped inside, following in the footsteps the team had obviously taken.

"They wouldn't want to give anyone in here time to react," Marco replied.

"I mean they didn't even try for a quiet entry," Maya said. "If there had been hostages, in a place this size... it could have gotten them killed."

As it was, though, the apartment block was almost eerily quiet in the wake of the raid. More doors hung open, showing where the SWAT team had rapidly cleared each room. Maya could see the marks of booted feet in the dust on the floor, showing them running from room to room, weapons ready.

The first one she looked in was empty except for a couple of old wooden pallets and a crate. There were old stains on the walls, but none of them looked new enough to matter.

"Maybe we'll get lucky," Marco said, as they moved on to another room, this one with stacks of old office furniture just left haphazardly. "Maybe the kidnapper will have left evidence here."

Maya wished she could feel that optimistic. If the kidnapper was careful enough to lay this trap in the first place, he was careful enough not to leave anything for them to find. In any case, a full SWAT team running through a building throwing flashbangs and battering down doors wasn't going to help with any trace evidence.

In spite of that, she made herself keep going. Maya had to see all this for herself.

116

She checked another room, this one with a series of chalk boards along the walls covered in doodles. Probably, someone was going to have to photograph each one and check if anything there had any relevance.

Not her, and not now, though.

Maya came to a set of stairs, leading both up into the rest of the apartment block and down into its basement.

"Up or down?" Marco asked.

Maya thought for a moment. Where would she have gone if she were the kidnapper? Where would be better to hold twelve women, assuming they'd ever been here? Would a man like that want the clear views of a higher floor, or the security of the basement?

"Down," Maya said at last, and set off into the basement. She took out her Glock even though the building had been cleared by SWAT, because in a place like this she was sure there would be plenty of nooks and crannies where someone might hide. The lights above were flickering and dim, so she took out a torch, holding it ready underneath the barrel of her sidearm.

She and Marco quickly found the spot where the SWAT team had run into a booby trap. There were scorch marks on one wall, and holes where projectiles had embedded themselves opposite.

"Some kind of improvised claymore mine?" Marco guessed.

Maya nodded. It was far too similar to the kind of IED she'd seen in the army for comfort.

"Do you think there are more?" Marco asked.

"SWAT wouldn't have sent us in here if they thought there were," Maya said, but despite that, she moved forward even more cautiously.

There was a large boiler room to her left, which again showed all the signs of being cleared by the team before her, but beyond that, the corridor wound on, and Maya kept following it.

"Are you sure this is the right way?" Marco asked.

Maya shook her head. "I'm not sure about anything right now, but the trap suggests that it might be."

"Unless he just left traps everywhere in the building."

There hadn't been any by the front door, though. Only here. So why? What was so important that it was worth protecting? Maya kept going. Ahead, there was what appeared to be a large open basement space, lit by a single shaky bulb that-

"Maya, wait," Marco said, and Maya froze.

She looked down. In spite of her caution, and the SWAT team's casual certainty that the building was clear, her leg was almost brushing up against the silvery length of a tripwire. Very carefully, she stepped back, then looked down its length. Another claymore was set there.

"I guess SWAT got out as soon as they started losing people," Maya said. Which meant that there might still be something deeper down here. Carefully, keeping her eyes on the ground, Maya stepped over the tripwire.

She moved into the space beyond, sweeping it for more traps, or for anyone waiting. Marco moved with her, gun ready, and he moved with a precision that Maya liked. It said that he'd done this enough times before that she could rely on him to do his part if this turned into a firefight.

"Clear," Maya said at last when it was obvious that there was no one there.

It was easy to tell, because the room was empty. Completely, utterly empty, save for a single chair set towards the back.

On that chair sat a rectangular card.

"No," Maya breathed, as she went forward.

The postcard had the familiar bunny design, although these ones looked sad rather than gamboling happily. Taking out evidence gloves, Maya lifted the postcard, turning it over so that she could read it. Just two words adorned its surface, and as she read those words, Maya's heart fell even further.

Dead End.

CHAPTER TWENTY

Maya felt as though the drive back took forever, and not just because Marco wasn't racing along at breakneck speed anymore. It was simply that every minute now was a minute taken away from the time she had left to finish the case, whereas before, it had been a minute closer to maybe seeing a conclusion to it.

It was probably only a couple of hours before Cleveland swung back into sight, but Maya felt as if she'd been cooped up in the car far longer.

"Back to the precinct?" Marco asked.

"Definitely." They needed to get back to it and try to make up for the time they'd just wasted. That the kidnapper had just *made* them waste. He'd punished their attempt to find him by making it so that Maya would waste hours on a raid that got them nothing. She was no further in finding him, and that much closer to the deadline.

"We'll find the killer in time," Marco said, obviously guessing what she was thinking. "Even if we have to work all night and all tomorrow, we'll do it."

Maya wished that she shared his confidence, but right then, the dead end of the abandoned apartment block had taken that certainty away from her. Even though she hadn't been the one to make the decision on the raid, it still felt like a symbol for all of this: a lot of effort, and nothing to be found at the end.

Still, there was something about Marco's determination that was infectious, making Maya want to keep going in spite of the setbacks. By the time they got back to Marco's precinct, she was only too ready to keep working through the files. They hurried towards the office, and Maya was halfway there before she saw the local police chief standing there in the office, waiting for them.

He was a large man of about fifty, resplendent in a uniform that was practically bursting at the seams with his bulk. He had bulldog features that were currently a deep shade of red, although that might have had something to do with how angry he obviously was.

"Get in here!" he snapped as Maya and Marco approached, loud enough that it carried around the bullpen. Maya saw several detectives look their way, and it seemed to her that they were enjoying this moment.

She and Marco went into the office, shutting the door behind them. Maya braced for what she suspected was going to come next.

"What do you think you're doing?" the chief demanded.

"Chief Linden-" Marco began, but the police chief obviously wasn't in a mood to let him talk.

"Shut up," the police chief snapped. "Do you think I want to listen to you when you've just gone against everything I've said and upset one of our most prominent citizens?"

One of their most prominent citizens?

"Do you mean Lucas McFadden?" Maya asked, laughing in spite of herself, barely able to believe that the dance coach could be described that way.

"You might think it's funny, Agent, but Lucas McFadden taught the mayor's daughter to dance, along with the kids of half the important people in Cleveland. Now you're going around questioning him and his students as if they're suspects, when everyone knows that Anne Postmartin was killed by the Moonlight Killer."

"We're following the evidence," Marco said, apparently trying to stand up for her.

"What evidence?" Chief Linden demanded. "What have you got that definitively points to McFadden? If there were any kind of smoking gun, it would have come up two years ago!"

"With respect," Maya said, because her bosses probably wouldn't want her calling a city police chief an idiot, "cold case work involves exploring possibilities that weren't run down in the original inquiry. Anne Postmartin was a dancer, in an environment where rivalries and resentment are common. Many of the dancers there were also her friends and can tell us more about her and what was going on around her than anyone else. It's only reasonable that I question the dance students. If McFadden doesn't like that, what is he trying to hide?"

"He's trying to protect a bunch of young women from FBI harassment, is what he's trying to do!" Chief Linden replied, not even beginning to calm down. "Do you know the crap I've had to put up with over all of this? The mayor doesn't like the case being reopened, because it brings back too much attention about the Moonlight Killer to the city. *I* don't like it being reopened by the FBI, because it's like you're saying that we can't do our jobs. It was bad enough when you all swept in last time. Doing it again makes us all look stupid."

120

"Not if we *catch* whoever did this," Marco said.

"And how likely is that, Spinelli?" Linden replied. "No, I'm done with this. No more warnings. Stay *away* from Lucas McFadden."

"This is an FBI case," Maya said.

"While you're investigating the Moonlight Killer, it is," Chief Linden said. "I can't stop you from going after a multi-state serial killer. But the moment you start treating it like a crime committed by a single killer in state, it's *our* jurisdiction. Back off from Lucas McFadden or I'll have you escorted from Cleveland, Agent, and I'll have your badge, Detective."

He turned and stalked from the office, slamming the door behind himself hard enough that Maya was surprised the glass didn't shatter. Maya could only stand there for several seconds afterwards, shaking with her own anger at being told to back off like that.

"What an asshole," she said, and she wasn't sure right then whether she meant Chief Linden, McFadden, or the mayor. Frankly, it could have applied to any of them.

Marco nodded. "This is a problem, though. If we can't look into the dance studio, then all the leads we were pursuing are dead."

"I know," Maya said. They'd committed to looking at Anne's personal life rather than at the Moonlight Killer angle. Now, it seemed as if that was being taken away from them. Without the chance to look at the dancers, she wasn't sure what they had.

"I'm going to call Deputy Director Harris," Maya said. "Maybe if I get him to talk to your police chief, it will get him to back off."

At the very least, it would remind him that the FBI were watching. It would buy her some time in which to solve this.

She called Harris's number and got through on the third ring.

"Gray," he said. "You calling to talk about how badly the raid went?"

He put it almost like she'd had some kind of say in whether it went ahead. She'd been the one arguing against it, but she knew better than to remind Harris of that immediately before she was about to ask for his help.

"No," Maya said. "I'm back in Cleveland, and they don't seem to want me to keep going with the lines of inquiry I'm looking at. They say I'm harassing prominent citizens."

"And are you?" Harris asked. That stopped Maya short, because it normally wouldn't have been the kind of question he would even have bothered asking.

"I'm trying to get to the truth of this," Maya said. "Wherever it leads."

"Well," Harris said, "maybe the time has come to stop."

That took Maya even more aback. Harris had never suggested stopping before a case was done, before.

"What?" Maya said.

"Gray, we've just thrown resources at a raid that was a total dead end," Harris said. The echo of the postcard's words was far too painful. "Except for injured officers. We're getting flak now from *two* local police forces, not to mention the Pittsburg FBI office. And all over what? A couple of postcards?"

"Twelve kidnapped women," Maya reminded him. "A threat to kill one if I don't solve this case."

"Assuming he has anyone," Harris said. "The current thinking here is that this is all a game to get us to go where he wants, and to hurt as many of us as possible."

"SWAT were only hurt because they charged in, trying to break this kidnapper's rules," Maya argued.

"We're the FBI," Harris said. "We don't give kidnappers or terrorists what they want."

"Terrorists?" Maya said, barely able to believe it.

"Like I said, the current thinking is that this is actually all about targeting police and FBI. From what I hear, you were pretty close to being killed yourself."

Someone had obviously told him about the second claymore.

"Even without all this, the Anne Postmartin case is a valid one," Maya said.

"You've said yourself that the Moonlight Killer probably isn't involved," Harris said. Maya could just imagine him sitting there in his big chair, trying to be reasonable. "That would make it a local matter."

It was uncomfortably close to what Chief Linden had said.

"And the threat to life?" Maya asked.

"Only applies if we believe that it's real," Harris replied. "I went along with the idea that it might be based on... what? A single postcard? Now, we've seen just how much this guy likes to mess with people, and the prevailing feeling here is that this case business is all a hoax, designed to waste your time, and make you jump through hoops for their amusement. Possibly there's even going to be an attempt to target you out of all this."

"The prevailing feeling, or just what Reyes thinks?" Maya asked, not really able to believe that Harris was going along with this. "What about the nickname he used on the postcard. The only way he would know that was if-"

"If he knew you really well, or if he knew Megan well, or if he got it from your social media somewhere," Harris said. "Maybe this is some ex-boyfriend trying to mess with you in a sick way, in which case, by all means, hunt him down on your own time."

"This isn't that and you know it," Maya snapped, starting to lose her temper. It was like Harris didn't trust her judgement anymore.

"What I know is that we've invested a lot of manpower and money into this," Harris said, "and all we've gotten back is embarrassment and people hurt. I don't want to give this guy what he wants by keeping you on this case. I'd rather spend my resources on catching him."

"Sir, I'm close on the Anne Postmartin case," Maya said. "There's only another day to the deadline anyway, and I really believe that we can get a result out of this."

"Close?" Harris said. "Do you have any concrete evidence? Any solid leads?"

"There's something going on at the dance academy," Maya said. "And if I can just-"

"No," Harris said. "I'm done playing into some hoaxer's hands. I should never have sent you out on this anyway, Gray. You're too close to all of this. A guy uses your sister, and suddenly you'll do anything he wants, even though there's no real chance that he *actually* has her."

"We don't know that," Maya said. She didn't want to back down on this. Yes, she wanted Megan to be safe, but she didn't think that this was a hoax. Her every instinct said that this was real. "Sir, I'm asking you to trust me."

"And on anything else, I would," Harris said. "But this is too personal for you to see straight. I'm pulling you from the case, Gray."

"No, you can't," Maya said, and instantly regretted it.

"Last I checked, I was your superior officer, Gray," Harris snapped back. "I want you back in DC, first thing tomorrow."

"Just one more day," Maya begged, and she had never thought that she would find herself begging over something like this.

"First thing tomorrow," Harris said, with no give in his voice. "If you aren't there, then it's going to be your career on the line."

He hung up and Maya stood there, blinking back the kind of tears she normally made a point of not shedding. She'd called Harris hoping

123

for support, and now it felt as if her entire world were crumbling underneath her. Harris was treating all this like it was a hoax, but Maya *knew* that her sister was in danger.

And now, if she didn't return to DC tomorrow, she was probably fired. What was she meant to do?

CHAPTER TWENTY ONE

Maya sat in the office, barely able to move, because she didn't know what she was going to do next. She was used to making life and death decisions in the heat of the moment, yet sitting here, like this, was harder.

"It will be ok, Maya," Marco tried, from across the office.

"How?" Maya replied, sharper than she intended. "How will this be ok?"

Her sister was in danger, and now her boss was telling her that she couldn't even keep going with the one thing that was keeping her safe. Maya wanted to keep going with this in spite of what Harris had said, but after what Marco's boss had threatened, there was no way that she could, was there? Even if she tried to throw away her career by continuing to investigate, then she had no doubt that Chief Linden would make good on his threat to throw her out of the city.

"We'll think of something," Marco said. "Are you worried about your job?"

She began to cry. The first few firefights she'd been in had knocked that out of her, teaching Maya to put up a hard shell that nothing reached through. Now, though, it felt as if all of that was falling away, leaving her vulnerable and unable to stop the sobs that wracked her.

Marco was there beside her instantly, putting an arm around her shoulders, holding onto her. Under other circumstances, Maya might have found herself responding to him being so close, but now she felt like a ball of spikes, barely able to let anyone close, let alone touch her.

"Maya," Marco said, "what is it? I know you want to save these women, but none of this is your fault. It isn't personal, it's the FBI and Chief Linden being assholes."

"One of those women is my sister!" Maya snapped at him, and only then realized what she'd said.

Marco was staring at her now, looking like he couldn't make sense of any of this. "Your sister?"

Maya didn't say anything for several seconds. She wasn't sure what to say, or how to explain this. A part of her just hoped that Marco would leave it, but a part of her wanted to explain it to him.

She realized that she didn't have to hold it back now. She was being thrown off the case anyway, so she didn't have to worry about everyone there thinking that she was too close to it. Why not tell the truth?

"The kidnapper has my sister."

She saw Marco's eyes widen as he started to understand what was going on. She could see him working through all her decisions over the last few days, seeing them again in the context of what he'd just heard.

"You're sure?" he said, after a few seconds.

Maya shook her head. "No, I'm not sure. I'm not sure about anything right now. But my sister has been missing for months now, and the postcard the guy sent used a nickname that Megan used to use for me."

That got another look of surprise from Marco.

"And your bosses aren't taking this *seriously*?" He sounded shocked.

Maya shook her head. She couldn't even find words now. She was too upset for it. She put her head down, trying to cover the tears that were flowing down her face. She hid away like that until she felt the weight of an arm around her shoulders. She looked up to find Marco holding her, just holding her, in a way that she never normally would have allowed. She was too tough for that, too in control.

Maya looked up at Marco, met his eyes, and found a connection there. There was something between them in that moment, something deep and consuming and electric. If this had been any other setting, Maya might have leaned in and kissed him right then. Only the presence of the bullpen just beyond the goldfish bowl of the office kept her from doing it now.

Even so, she stared at him, caught between what she wanted to do and what she knew she should do. It was far too close to the situation she was in with the case. There was what she should do as an agent, and then there was what she wanted to do as a person, as someone who wanted to solve the case, as a *sister.*

She kept staring at Marco, and the moment stretched, and stretched, and…

A fist hammering on the door broke the moment apart, causing her and Marco to jump back from one another. Maya wiped her eyes hurriedly as the door opened, letting in a uniformed officer.

126

"I didn't want to interrupt while the chief was in here," the officer said. "But a package came for you, dropped off by courier at the front desk."

"A package for me?" Marco said. "Who's sending me packages at work?"

"Not you, Detective Spinelli," the officer said. "For Agent Gray."

That caught Maya off guard. Who even knew that she was there? Only one person that she could think of.

"Did you see where the package came from?" she asked.

The uniformed officer shrugged. "A courier brought it to the front desk. Probably there's a trail there, if you want to follow it."

She held out her hand for the package, and the officer passed it over. It was bound up in brown paper and string, and there was a postcard taped to the front of it, with an all too familiar bunny motif on the front of it.

Maya's heart was in her mouth as she took the package.

She knew that standard procedure would be to test the package fully for contaminants and explosives. *Especially* after what had happened at the abandoned building in Pittsburg. The presence of the postcard took away all of that caution, though. She snatched up the postcard, turning it over to read the words that were there.

This is the bunny who will die if you fail to meet the deadline. Solve the case, Agent Gray. Stop wasting time chasing me. The injured agents are payment enough for this one, but next time, a bunny will pay the price. You'll only hit dead ends.

Maya read the postcard through again. One obvious point struck her: the kidnapper knew about the raid. This had been sent in response to the raid, which meant that the kidnapper had been watching somehow.

She tore open the package.

There was a yellow blouse inside, in pieces, as if it had been cut away from someone. Maya wanted to take it in her hands, but then realized that she would only be contaminating the evidence if she did so.

Looking at it, she realized two things: first, she might actually have evidence that the kidnapper had taken women.

Second, there was no way that Maya was going to give up on the case now.

"Marco," she said. "Do you think that you can get this pushed through forensics? Do you think you can run the DNA?"

Marco nodded. "I know someone in the labs who owes me a favor."

*

Maya couldn't hide her frustration as she stood in the police forensics lab, waiting while a woman in a white coat stood over a machine. She was about thirty, with short blonde hair, strong features, and glasses.

"How much longer is this going to take?" Maya asked, not able to help herself. They'd been waiting around for a good couple of hours now.

The woman looked up at her with obvious dislike.

"These things take time, Agent. I've already skipped you ahead of a bunch of other work. There are plenty of other urgent cases, you know."

"But how much time, Charlotte?" Marco asked.

The forensic scientist beamed over at him, her whole demeanor changing.

"Not much longer, Marco. Soon."

The difference was marked, and Maya could tell without asking any questions exactly why the forensic scientist was so much friendlier with Marco. She liked him, in a way that was completely obvious to Maya, but which Marco seemed slightly oblivious to.

Maybe he didn't notice the effect he was having. Maybe he *didn't* notice just how good looking he was, or the attention that he attracted. He'd flirted with Maya as naturally as breathing. Maybe it didn't mean anything.

Maya wanted to believe that it did, but at the same time, maybe it was better if it didn't. It would make things a lot simpler, once she had to leave.

For now, though, there was only the frustration of having to wait, both for the forensic results and possibly with Marco. Maya couldn't even wander around the lab, looking for something to do, because she suspected that would only give Charlotte from forensics an excuse to pick a fight with her.

"Ok," Charlotte said. "I've isolated the DNA. I just need to run it through the database. If this is from a missing person, there's a good chance DNA will be on file."

She went over to a computer, where a large screen flickered through faces and files. Even with the time she'd spent looking for

128

Megan, Maya hadn't realized that so many people were missing. Woman after woman flashed past, each one representing a family left worrying, a life suddenly vacated, the possibility of a body being found one day, the victim of a crime.

Maybe there wouldn't be a match. Not everyone sent a DNA sample for comparison to the databases. Some people didn't have family or friends to do that kind of thing for them. Some people were left with just the kind of anonymous disappearance that meant that they would never be found, never be remembered.

"I have a match," Charlotte said, as the computer behind her stabilized with the face of a white, blonde haired young woman. "This clothing belongs to Liza Carty, who went missing in New York three months ago."

Maya stared at that image, and she was ashamed of the first thought that came into her head, because that first thought was gratitude that she now had proof. Almost as soon as the image stabilized in front of her, she had her phone out, calling Harris's number.

He waited seven rings before he picked up. Maya guessed that he was deciding whether he needed the argument or not.

"Gray, if this is you calling to try to argue for more time-"

"I've had a package from the kidnapper," Maya said, because it seemed like the only way to grab her boss's attention right then.

"Gray, we've been through this. It's designed to manipulate you."

"That package contained clothing that I've just had DNA matched to a missing woman," Maya continued. "Liza Carty, from New York. The kidnapper has gotten in touch, and he has provided evidence that he not only has women in captivity, but that he intends to kill a specific target if I fail to solve this case."

There was silence on the end of the phone for so long that Maya almost though that Harris had hung up.

"Well, shit," he said, after what seemed like an eternity. "Gray, if you're making this up-"

"I'm not," Maya said. "I have the DNA right here. I have evidence that whoever sent the postcard actually has women captive somewhere. Which means that, manipulation or not, the threat is real. If I don't solve this case, then at least one woman is going to die."

"I know what it means," Harris said. "I'm just trying to work out what to do about it."

There was no question about what to do in Maya's mind. They'd already proven that they couldn't just find this guy.

"Sir, you *know* what to do," she said. "This woman's only hope is if I solve this case, but I can't do that with Cleveland PD on my back, complaining because I've upset their prominent citizens."

"Which means that I have to call Chief... Linden, was it?"

"Yes," Maya confirmed.

"I have to call him and tell him that this is an FBI matter, because it relates to multiple kidnappings across multiple states."

"Yes, sir," Maya said.

There was another pause, almost as long as the first. "All right. I'll call him. And Gray?"

"Yes, sir?" Maya said. She wasn't expecting an apology, which was probably just as well.

"Make sure you solve this."

CHAPTER TWENTY TWO

Maya all but ran back to the office she shared with Marco. Just like that, Maya was back on the case, but now she needed to work out what she was going to do to actually *crack* the case in the brief time she had left. Going to Pittsburg and back had taken so much time out of today that it felt as if they were running to catch up now even more than before.

She passed Chief Linden on the way up. He was currently on the phone and looking sheepish. Apparently, Deputy Director Harris worked fast.

"Looks like you get to keep going," he snapped at them as Maya headed for the office, "but don't think I'm going to forget this, Spinelli."

Maya felt a little bad in that moment. She might be on the case again, but she'd probably bought Marco a world of trouble.

"And I'm not going to forget that you tried to stop us from actually catching a murderer, sir," Marco shot back, loud enough that the rest of the bullpen could hear. Chief Linden looked, if anything, even more sheepish than he had before. Maya got the impression that people didn't stand up to him very often.

"Where do you want to start?" Marco asked as soon as they were back in the office. "Do we keep going down the list of dancers?"

A part of Maya wanted to go visit every one of them, but she could guess how much time that would take, and how much pushback they would get from Lucas McFadden's friends. Not that Maya cared about that part.

"We find numbers for them and call them," Maya said, taking out the list, "but we'll have to leave out going to them physically. It just takes too long, when they're just blanking us."

"It will be harder to see if they're lying about something," Marco pointed out.

Maya shook her head. "The research says people identify lies better by voice alone than by body language. Besides, we already know that there's something off in the dance studio. It's just a question of finding the one girl willing to talk about *what*."

"You're still convinced that the answer's there?" Marco asked.

Maya hesitated, sitting back in her chair within their shared office and taking up another of the files on the case.

"I don't know," she said. "It feels like I've been locked onto it pretty tightly, the last day or so. I want to look through everything again and see what else there might be to find. So far, it seems like everybody has an alibi, or they didn't have a real reason to hurt Anne, or I just don't believe that they could have been the one to do it."

They needed something new, but that was the problem with cold cases: there was very little new to be found, just new ways of piecing together old evidence. Even so, Maya plunged back into the stack of files, reading and re-reading, hoping that something would stand out to her as Marco started making the calls.

"Hello, is that Imogen? This is Detective Spinelli of the Cleveland PD. I was hoping to talk to you about Anne Postmartin."

Maya dug into a file that had looked into Anne's progress at college. She had decent grades, nothing to mark her out as in trouble academically, no sudden change in their pattern that might suggest something unusual going on in her life. If anything, her grades had drifted up very slightly in the weeks before her death, but that might just be down to not spending all her time training for dancing.

"Yes," Marco said. "I know it's been a long time, but anything you can tell me might help. Did Anne have any enemies? Any rivals at the dance school who hated her guts? No?"

Maya found her mind skipping back to those absences that no one seemed to be able to explain.

"Ask about a boyfriend," she said.

Marco raised an eyebrow. "We're back on that?"

"We're back on *everything*," Maya said. There was no time now to pick one theory over another. They just had to grind away at everything, hoping that something gave, that something sparked a moment of connection in Maya's head.

"Imogen," Marco said. "Do you know if Anne had a boyfriend? Not that you knew of? Well, was there anything else? Anything strange going on at the dance studio that... she hung up."

"Keep trying," Maya said. In its way, hanging up said as much as the sudden silences in the conversations had when they'd been talking to the dancers face-to-face. There was something there, but Maya knew that she couldn't throw her full energy at it now, and risk missing something else.

What else, though? Why were murders committed? Maya knew the answers to that as well as anyone, and the problem was that it didn't have to be something big. Money, jealousy, sex, power were all common enough, but what if Anne had just looked at someone the wrong way? Made the wrong comment at the wrong time and found herself on the receiving end of someone else's hatred without even knowing it?

No, Maya couldn't think like that. She had to believe that there was something to this that she might be able to find. She had to believe that there was some kind of reason to this, and that the kidnapper wouldn't have thrown her at the case without there being at least a *chance* for Maya to solve it.

"Why did the kidnapper send the clothes?" Maya asked.

"To keep you on the case," Marco replied. "To provide proof that there really are women there, at his mercy."

"What if it's more than that, though?" Maya suggested. "I mean, why Liza Carty, and not someone else? He's shown that he's good at embedding clues in other things, with Anne's name as the sender for the first postcard, and the fake trail to the empty building."

"He's also shown that he likes to mess with people's heads," Marco said. "It might not mean anything."

Maya felt sure that there had to be some kind of connection, though, so she hit her computer, trying to find any information she could on Liza Carty. Because she'd been a missing person, and because her family had filed a report, that information was easy enough to locate.

Liza Carty was twenty-one, the age Anne would have been now. Looking at her picture, Maya could see some similarities in their features, their blonde haired, clean cut good looks. Was that deliberate?

Maya started to read through Liza's missing person file, then decided to go further and looked up her social media accounts. Those were still active, not archived the way they might have been if she'd been confirmed dead, but the last posts were from a couple of months back.

Maya stared as she began to scroll through the last few posts. It reminded her of searching through her sister's accounts, trying to find clues to where she might be. It reminded her of more than that, though.

It reminded her of Anne.

There were videos of Liza Carty on stage, singing. Maya was no judge of that kind of thing, but it seemed to her that Liza had a good voice, and a natural flair for performing. Certainly, there were plenty of likes on each of her posts, suggesting that at least some people thought she was good. Even looking at the videos, Maya could see the size of the audiences in bars and clubs, looking as though Liza Carty had the talent to draw a crowd.

The thing that clinched it, though, was one post from just a couple of weeks before Liza had disappeared.

Can't say much, very hush hush, but I'm in talks with a major label. A MAJOR LABEL! We're going places, people!

The similarity was too much to ignore. Two young women around the same age, both performers, both on the cusp of things that might have propelled them to national attention. Was that what all this was about? Was it about performers? Megan had wanted to go to art school. Had that been enough to put her in the kidnapper's line of fire?

Would following *that* angle get Maya the answers she needed?

That was the problem: the more she looked at this, the harder it was to believe that the two were truly linked. Liza had been taken from New York. Anne had been killed in Cleveland. They had almost certainly never met, and even if they had, did that tell Maya anything about Anne's killer?

Maybe not, but perhaps it told her something about the man who'd kidnapped her sister. He'd taken a singer and sent her to look into the killer of a dancer. He clearly had some kind of interest in performers. Perhaps he was one himself.

Another possibility came to Maya: perhaps his interest in performers was in hurting them. Maybe he'd sent her to look into Anne's death with the idea of producing proof that *he* had committed the crime, not the Moonlight Killer. Maybe this was him trying to claim *credit*.

That was a sickening thought, because of what it might mean for those he'd kidnapped. Would he really keep his word, given the chance to kill them?

"Got something?" Marco asked.

"Just that the kidnapped woman and Anne are both performers," Maya said. "But I'm not sure that it gets us any closer to the truth."

"And the calls to the dancers aren't going much better," Marco said.

"We keep going," Maya said. "There has to be *something* that we can find."

She dove into the files again, reading through witness statements from the time. Maya started to draw out a map of the beachfront and its stage, trying to work out exactly where everyone had been. It was painstaking work, going through each witness statement and trying to place people's movements over the course of the evening when Anne had died. The dancers said that they'd all stayed together, and gone in pairs when they'd gone anywhere, for safety. Lucas McFadden said that he'd been in sight of the teardown crew after the performance. Dane Carlucci had been at a club.

Where was the person who was out of place? Maya kept drawing, sketching patterns of movement, times, people. If Maya could find even a few minutes when someone wasn't watched by someone else...

She could feel her eyes starting to close. It had been a long day and driving to Pittsburg and back hadn't helped. She forced herself to keep going anyway, picking out another witness statement, making a few more marks on the map...

*

Maya blinked, opening her eyes. There was daylight filtering into the office, rather than its usual electric light. She was sitting at her desk, her neck ached, and she more or less had to peel her face from the map. In the morning light, she wasn't quite sure that she remembered what all the marks meant.

Marco was there, putting a cup of coffee down in front of her.

"I fell asleep," she said.

She saw Marco nod.

"Why did you let me sleep?" Maya demanded. "I could have-"

"You couldn't have done any more than you did," Marco said. "And if you're exhausted enough to sleep in a busy precinct, you're exhausted enough that you need the sleep. I kept going for a while, making the rest of the calls."

"And?" Maya asked. She took the coffee. It was bitter enough to wake her up, at least.

Marco shook his head. "Nothing we haven't heard."

Which left them where? With a link between the killing and the kidnapper that might or might not be relevant. With plenty of potential suspects, if only they could find one who seemed to actually hate Anne enough to kill her, and who didn't have an alibi. With piles of information relating to Anne, there was no way of knowing if anything was relevant.

135

Crucially, the morning light meant one other thing: they were running out of time. It was the morning of the 29th. They had less than twenty-four hours to solve the case now, or Liza Carty was going to die.

CHAPTER TWENTY THREE

Frank sat on a chair at the heart of his bunker, with eleven of his bunnies clustered around, looking everything from scared to resigned to defiant. Thanks to the coveralls he'd given them, they all had a sameness to them that he enjoyed. He enjoyed the looks of fear, too, and the knowledge that he was the one with the power to make them feel that.

Frank sat there watching them, watching their reactions. After what had happened with Liza Carty, none of them seemed inclined to rebel again. That was almost a pity. There was something quite satisfying about keeping his bunnies in their place.

The room he was in was large and mostly empty, except for a dozen portraits set out around the walls, each one representing one of the women there. Of course, in the portraits, they had bunny ears and little bunny noses, but he felt that added to the likenesses, rather than detracting. They were all scared as rabbits in any case.

Perhaps, he thought, he should have given their outfits little bunny tails, but that might have been a hint of whimsy too far. Besides, Frank suspected that anyone buying a dozen such things in the last few months might attract attention, now that the FBI were looking for him.

"You're all scared," Frank said, from behind his mask. He didn't remove it down here, because if one of them saw his face, he would have to kill her there and then. That would ruin his game. "That's good. That's the way things *should* be."

He went over to the portrait of Liza Carty. It had a little board with facts about her below it. All the portraits did, wanting to make it clear to Frank's bunnies that he knew them, that he'd taken the *time* to know them. He wanted them to know the care that he'd taken over them, and how important that should make them feel to him.

Slowly, carefully, he took the portrait down. One way or another, Liza would be leaving soon.

Going from the main room, Frank went through into the space where Liza Carty still hung by her hands in the killing circle, locking the door behind himself. She was whimpering now, going from a position where she had to take her weight on her tiptoes to one where her arms had to take her weight.

"They say that the stresses of being left in a position like that are immense," Frank said, moving close to her, observing the rapid rise and fall of her breathing, the quivering of her muscles. "It can kill, if left long enough. But it would not be a punishment for trying to escape if it were easy. And, of course, the FBI earned you more punishment the moment they tried to catch me."

Frank turned his back on her for now, going to the screens. He checked that the bugs he had near Agent Gray were working. Dear Maya, so easy to check up on. It was important, Frank had found, to make sure that he knew as much as he could. He liked games, but it was important to make sure that he won them. For now, there was no camera he could access that had a line of sight on her, so he had to make do with listening.

Even that was made less than ideal by the continued sounds of discomfort from the bunny behind him.

"Quiet!" Frank snapped at her, looking round with a glare that stunned her into silence in spite of his mask.

She couldn't stay silent for long, though, and soon, Liza Carty was moaning again.

"If you can't be quiet, then at least sing for me," Frank said, standing and going to her. "That's what you're meant to be good at, isn't it? Singing? Sing for me. *Now.*"

She tried. Frank could hear her trying, with a version of *Amazing Grace* that he'd heard her use on some talent show or other. There was, he had to admit, a kind of beauty to her voice, although it wasn't helped by the tremble of fear in it, or by the stress of her current predicament.

Frank joined in, with the rolling tenor he'd taken the time to perfect, letting the notes ring out around the room they were in. A private performance, just for the two of them, since the soundproofing of this room prevented anyone else from hearing. No one could hear even the loudest scream in here. Frank knew that for a fact.

Eventually, Liza Carty's voice gave out into sobs, and Frank kept going, performing for her, switching into a show tune and adding in a few polished steps to go with it. Frank let the last notes fade and took a moment to enjoy the small triumph of out-singing this would-be star.

Taking a bottle, he gave Liza a sip of water.

"There," he said. "That wasn't so bad, was it?"

She'd earned that much with her performance, if nothing else. When he was sure that she'd drunk enough that she would be able to keep going, Frank turned her almost gently towards the spot where the clock sat above the screens, still counting down in large lines of red. The numbers were getting lower now.

"Less than a day, Liza," Frank said. "Are you an optimist? That's what you say on all your social media profiles; that if you think good things, good things will happen. So shall *we* think good things? Less than a day until dear Maya does what I've asked her to do, and you get to go free."

"Please, please don't hurt me!" Liza managed, in between the beginnings of sobs. Ah, Frank thought. Not such an optimist after all.

"Oh, you don't like that way of thinking about it?" Frank said. "Well, maybe we'll put it the other way, then. Less than a day. Midnight tonight, and if Maya hasn't done what I require of her, then we'll find all kinds of other ways to make you sing out before you die."

CHAPTER TWENTY FOUR

Time was running out, and Maya still didn't know which way to go with the case. It felt as though she'd looked at every angle, tried every hypothesis, and nothing had quite fit. She needed to find something *new*.

She tried looking down at the chart she'd made, but even after taking the time to try to unravel it while Marco brought coffee and bagels, it didn't tell her much. If the witness statements could be believed, then everyone was accounted for during the period when the coroner said Anne was killed.

It couldn't be any of her friends, who were all together. It couldn't even be Lucas McFadden, as much as Maya wanted it to be. Maybe it was Dane Carlucci after all, but no, if he was going to kill anyone, it would have been the girl he'd been harassing.

She called the club he'd mentioned, Spiders, just in case.

"Hi," she said when someone picked up. "My name is Maya Gray, I'm with the FBI cold cases unit. I'm calling about-"

"Dane Carlucci," a man's voice said, before Maya could finish.

That caught Maya by surprise, until she realized what must have happened. "He called you?"

"He said you would probably show up, or call. He wanted us to go back through our camera footage to try to find images of him from two years ago. I told him what I'll tell you: we don't keep it that long."

Which sounded like Dane didn't have an alibi, except for one thing. "He asked you to find footage? Not just to provide him with an alibi?"

"Yes, ma'am."

It wasn't any kind of proof, but why would Dane do that unless he thought that there might be footage to find? Maya had half expected to run into a suddenly perfect fake alibi, and that would have been suspicious in itself, but no. Instead, she'd found a young man trying to find real proof that he was in the place he'd said he was.

That didn't strike Maya as the action of someone who was lying about where he was.

"Ok, thank you," Maya said, and hung up.

Still nothing. Was there anything in the connection between the kidnapped woman and Anne? Could the kidnapper really be the killer? Could this just be about a serial killer not wanting the Moonlight Killer to get credit for what he'd done?

No, if that had been the case, surely he would have just claimed credit for it?

Maya got up and started pacing the office. Back in the army, they'd said that there was always a way to get the mission done, if you were willing to think unconventionally enough. So what wasn't she thinking about here?

"Maya?" Marco said, stepping in front of her. "Are you ok?"

"Why can't I think, Marco?" Maya asked. "Why can't I work this out?"

She wasn't used to not being able to work out a case. Normally, she had the near certainty that if she only put in enough time, she would be able to get somewhere. Her clean up rate spoke for itself. Yet here, there was no time. She couldn't just grind this down.

"You've already done more than any of the other FBI agents managed," Marco pointed out. "You're the first one to not just focus on the Moonlight Killer. You're the first one who really put Anne at the heart of this."

Anne. This was all about Anne Postmartin. There was *something* in her life that had led to this. If this started with her, then maybe Maya needed to look at her life again. What was there in her life that might explain any of this? What was there in her life that didn't fit.

Maya went back to Anne's file, starting to read through. Anne Postmartin, the dancer, who'd been going to community college, and-

Wait.

Community college?

"Marco, why was Anne going to community college?" Maya asked.

"What?" Marco said.

"Why was she going to the local community college?" Maya asked again. "Her grades were ok, and she had this skill at a national, even international, level. Imagine if she'd been a football player."

Maya saw the moment when Marco started to understand, in the slight widening of his eyes.

"She'd have been snapped up by a major university," Marco said. "Ivy league or something. But would that happen with dance?"

"There are plenty of specialist arts colleges," Maya pointed out. "And a few of the big universities have dance programs. Someone like

Anne should have been able to walk into one of them, probably with a full-ride scholarship."

"So why didn't she?" Marco said.

Maya nodded. "That's the question. What did she stay for? What, or who?"

"I don't think anyone bothered to ask that question before," Marco said, and Maya could hear the excitement in his voice.

She understood it, because she had the same excitement. For pretty much the first time in this case, she wasn't going over old ground, wasn't about to run into an alibi that had already been there for two years.

Maybe this was the angle they needed. Maybe this was the way that they were going to break open the case.

"How do we find out, though?" Marco said. "How do we work out if this is relevant?"

"We go back to see Anne Postmartin's parents."

*

When they got back to Anne's house, Maya noted that one of the cars wasn't in the driveway. She guessed that Jon Postmartin was out at work. Maybe that would play in their favor.

Tami Postmartin must have seen them coming up the driveway because, she opened the door as they approached. She didn't look happy to see them.

"What are you doing back here?" she demanded. "Jon has been in pieces since you came by. Do you understand the damage you've done?"

So much for this being easier with Jon Postmartin out.

"Tami-" Marco began, but Tami Postmartin cut him off.

"Don't you 'Tami' me. You're as bad as she is. All you care about is getting the glory from solving a case. You're not the one who has to live with the aftermath of everyone's lives being disrupted. You don't know what it's like."

Except that Maya *did* know what it was like, and not just because she'd seen exactly that kind of disruption in the cold cases she'd worked. Her sister had been missing for months, and now that something had finally changed, now that she finally had an idea where Megan might be, it was worse, not better.

142

"It's like you lose everything in those first few days," Maya said, half closing her eyes. "You're panicking, but you can't find anything to do that will help. You try to trust the police to do their jobs, but when nothing works, you trust them less, and less. You can't get any kind of closure because you don't have any kind of answers. For a while, you tell yourself that's all you need."

Maya could see the look of surprise in Tami's eyes. She could also see Marco watching her, looking worried now that he knew Maya's secret. Maya kept going anyway.

"Then time passes, and you still don't get answers," Maya said, "so you have to go on with your normal life anyway. People are sympathetic, but for them, it's just a thing that happened in the past, and they cut you less and less slack if you don't behave 'normally.' So you start to re-build what you think is a normal life. You find ways to cope, even if it's not normal. You build a life, scab the wound over."

That was the place Maya had been starting to get to before the postcard had come. She'd still been searching desperately for her sister, but there had also been that part of her that had been building up a routine around it, doing things the same way every day.

She could see the sympathy on Marco's face now, and Maya had to work to ignore it. She couldn't focus on that now, or she would break down, and Tami Postmartin would know far more about Maya than Maya wanted her to know.

"Then something comes that breaks you out of that, and you realize that none of it was normal," Maya said. "It's like ripping off bandages only to realize that the wound is still wide open. But that's what you have to do if you *actually* want things to heal. It's also what has to happen if we want to actually *catch* Anne's killer."

Tami stared at her, and Maya thought she saw tears glistening in the other woman's eyes.

"How… how do you know all that?" Tami asked. "Something they teach you in the FBI?"

"Something like that," Maya said, because there was no way she was going to reveal the real reason. "But right now, I know that there are things about Anne's life that no one thought to ask in the original inquiry."

Even then, she thought that Tami might not let them in, but then she relented, stepping back. She waved Maya and Marco through to the sitting room, and once again, they found themselves perched on that cream-colored furniture.

"What is it you want to know?" Tami asked.

"This is going to sound odd," Maya said, "but why did Anne go to community college?"

"You want to ask me *that?*" Tami said, clearly confused. "I mean, it was just where she wanted to go."

"But why?" Maya insisted. "Did she have chances to go anywhere else?"

Tami still seemed puzzled, but she at least took the time to think about it.

"I *think* there was an offer to go to Columbia, over in New York. I know Jon was really excited about the quality of their dance program. But then, she decided that she didn't want to go all the way to New York."

Maya saw Marco take out his phone, and she *knew* he was looking up Columbia's dance program.

"Tami," he said, after a moment or two. "Columbia's dance program is reckoned to be the best in the country. Anne passed that up?"

"I... guess," Tami said. She sounded as if she didn't understand it either now. "I think she just wanted to be closer to home. She liked things around here."

That didn't sound quite right, either. Anne was building up towards the possibility of fame, and an international career. Both would involve her traveling around the world. It didn't fit with the idea of a young woman who wanted to stay in Cleveland and go to the local college. Even here, there should have been plenty of options, but she'd gone for a small community college. Why there?

Who was going to that college that Anne wanted to be near?

"Tami, can I look at Anne's high school yearbook?"

"I... guess. It's in the cabinet."

Maya went over to the cabinet where Anne's parents had collected together all her trophies. There, at the back, she spotted the high school yearbook. Taking it out, Maya started to leaf through the rows of photographs, most of them signed, with small messages. Anne was pretty popular.

"What are you looking for, Maya?" Marco asked.

"I'll tell you when I... there."

She held up the yearbook so that Marco would be able to see. Hewitt James, a square jawed, handsome boy, had his picture circled

144

with a heart, shot through with an arrow with an A and a H on either side. The words "Love, always" stood below.

Maya knew the reason now why Anne had gone to community college. She was willing to bet that, when she looked, that would be exactly where Hewitt James had gone.

"We've found him," Maya said, barely able to believe it. "I knew he was out there somewhere, and we've found him. The missing boyfriend, Marco."

Maya checked her watch. They were running out of time. They *had* to find Hewitt James.

CHAPTER TWENTY FIVE

Maya all but ran back to the Explorer, getting out her phone and using its screen to start the search for Hewitt James. In the driver's seat, she could see Marco starting to do the same. Now that they had a name for Anne's mysterious boyfriend, they needed to know everything about him.

They could have gone back to the office for this, but that would have taken extra time, and right then, Maya didn't feel as though they had any time to spare.

The first thing she did was to search Anne's social media. There was no Hewitt James following her that Maya could see, but that might just mean that he'd used a handle that didn't link to his name. Or maybe he'd just been cautious. Maybe there had been a reason that he hadn't wanted people to know that he was seeing Anne.

That raised a few flags in itself. What kids their age weren't all over each other's posts, making it completely public what they felt for one another?

"Got something," Marco said. "This is the kid from the yearbook, right?"

He held out his phone for Maya to see, and sure enough, Hewitt James was there looking out at her.

"That's him," Maya confirmed.

"Well, it turns out that he has a record," Marco said.

Anne's boyfriend was getting more interesting by the moment, as far as Maya was concerned.

"For what?" she asked. Would there be anything there that was obvious precursor to violence?

"Small stuff, mostly," Marco said. "Vandalism, petty theft, the usual things you see with kids who are growing up to be troublemakers."

"I *don't* see it," Maya reminded him. The FBI didn't see kids like Hewitt James, unless they graduated to more serious things. "You'll have to tell me, Marco. How bad is this kid?"

She saw Marco shrug. "Hard to say," he said. "I'd say typical problem kid. Nothing bad enough to get him thrown in juvie for long, but no sign that he was changing his behavior either."

"A real bad boy," Maya said, imagining how it must have gone. Anne, the straightlaced dancer who worked hard for everything and never missed a practice session met Hewitt, the good-looking bad boy who didn't follow any rules. Soon, Anne was skipping out on her friends and her training to see him, and even turned down an offer from Columbia to make sure she stayed near him.

No wonder it had been so hard to find out about Anne's boyfriend. This was one boy Anne would have had to keep a secret. Probably, that was part of the thrill.

"Can you find an address for him?" Maya asked.

"Working on it," Marco said, tapping away. Maya caught the look of triumph in his eyes as he found something. "He used to live here in Cleveland. Now he lives in Columbus, at an address probably a couple of hours from here. But guess when he moved?"

Maya could feel her excitement building at the possibility that they were onto something. "Right after the murder?"

"Less than a month after."

Maya could feel the case starting to break open, could feel the first glimmers of light there at the end of the tunnel.

"Marco, we need to get to Columbus. Now."

*

Hewitt James' apartment building wasn't quite as run down as the abandoned one the kidnapper had led them to, but to Maya, it didn't seem far off. The fire escapes were rusted. The dumpsters out back were covered in graffiti. She could see a couple of kids eyeing them suspiciously as they drove up, then walking off hurriedly.

"This is the kind of place where I'm glad I don't drive a nicer looking car," Marco said. "You go in to talk to a suspect. You come out and your car's been stolen."

Maya could feel the anticipation building as she and Marco headed into the apartment building. The elevator was broken, so they took the stairs up to the third floor, with Maya trying to ignore the scent of something rotten in the stairwell.

Three-B was meant to be Hewitt James' current address. Maya stepped up next to the door and found herself checking that she had

147

easy access to her gun. Every instinct she had said that this had the potential to turn dangerous.

She knocked on the door. There was no answer.

She knocked again, harder this time. "Hewitt James? Open up, this is the police!"

Maya heard something beyond the door, the sound of someone moving, and the scrape of a window that hadn't been opened in a long time.

"He's running!" Maya called out even as she stepped back and kicked the door. It held against the first kick, but her second broke it open. Maya had a second to take in a dingy apartment with a few cheap pieces of furniture, but her gaze was focused on the far side of the place.

Hewitt James was there, in the middle of climbing out of a window onto the fire escape beyond. He was a little older looking than his picture, lean, wearing a hooded top and jeans, with a scruffy beard now that didn't suit him.

"Freeze, Hewitt!" Maya called out.

He didn't listen, instead leaping out through the window. Maya heard the clatter of his feet on the metal fire escape.

"Marco, take the stairs, cut him off!" Maya yelled back, even as she sprinted across the room after the fleeing young man.

She threw herself through the window, out onto the fire escape. It was better to move fast now than to clamber through carefully. Slow would give Hewitt a chance to attack her if he was waiting in ambush. Fast gave her a chance to surprise him.

So Maya plunged through, hitting the fire escape hard and coming up ready to fight if she had to. Hewitt wasn't there, though, already making his way down the fire escape to the floor below.

Maya set off in pursuit, running down the stairs, cornering as quickly as she could. She saw Hewitt kick the ladder for the escape free below, then set off down it at speed, sliding down.

Maya slid down the ladder after him, and only realized as she hit the ground that Hewitt was running in the opposite direction to the entrance, away down an alley.

"Marco, this way!" she called out, in case he could hear her, but there was no time in which to wait for him. All she could do was run after Hewitt, making sure that she kept him in sight and didn't give him a chance to get away.

He was fast, running with a lean, loping stride that covered the ground as he dodged around dumpsters. Maya saw him grab hold of a garbage can and was already sidestepping as he flung it into her path, not slowing down.

Hewitt kept running, taking a turn down another alley. There were a couple of motorbikes parked there, and Hewitt knocked those over into Maya's path as he had the garbage can. She hurdled them and kept chasing.

Hewitt was running well. Maya suspected that he ran a lot, because most suspects were out of breath well before now. Even so, she was keeping pace. She was used to chasing. She was *good* at chasing.

Hewitt slipped through a gate in a chain link fence, slammed it behind himself, and there was a padlock there that he slipped into place. It meant that Maya had to clamber over it, and even as she did it, Hewitt was sprinting away again.

He took another turn as Maya landed, and for a moment or two, he was out of sight. Maya landed hard, ran forward, and skidded around the corner. Hewitt was increasing his lead now and had already made it to another turn in what appeared to be a maze of back alleys.

Maya wasn't going to let him go that easily, though. She wasn't about to let such a clear suspect in Anne's murder get away, not when they wouldn't have the time to find him again. She ran around the corner and froze. Hewitt James was no longer in sight, in an alley that was empty except for another couple of dumpsters, a small nook that had steps down to the basement level of a building, and a rusted-out car.

Maya's first instinct was to keep running forward, making sure that she kept pace with Hewitt wherever he'd gone. Maya overruled that instinct, because the alley was too long for him to have made it to the end without her at least catching a glimpse of him.

He was still here, somewhere.

"Come out, Hewitt," Maya said, drawing her sidearm and holding it tight to her. "I know you're here somewhere. Come out with your hands up. You're under arrest."

Running had clinched that part. He'd been suspicious enough before, but the moment he'd run, Maya had known that she and Marco would be bringing him in. Now all she had to do was actually *catch* him.

Maya checked the space behind the dumpsters, moving carefully, trying to catch any glimpse of Hewitt she could before she finally leapt

149

out with her weapon drawn. She found herself pointing it at empty space, and now her quarry was down to just two hiding spots.

Maya went to the stairwell next, guessing that Hewitt might be down there, trying to work out a way to get into the basement beyond and get away. She hadn't heard the sound of a door being opened, though, so she was pretty sure that he was still there.

She braced herself, swung into place at the top of the steps, and stared down. Nothing, which left only…

Maya heard the scuff of someone running forward, and she started to turn. She was too late, because Hewitt James was almost on top of her, shoving Maya as hard as he could. Maya felt herself lose her balance, and she knew that his plan then was simple: push her down the steps and run while she recovered.

Maya did the only thing she could think of to stop that plan: she grabbed onto Hewitt's hooded top and pulled him with her.

They went tumbling down the steps towards the basement together. Maya felt stone steps slam into her side and then her back with jarring force, but she managed to keep tucked so that her head didn't hit on them. Somehow, she managed to keep her grip on the Glock, but that just meant that she had to fight to keep from accidentally shooting Hewitt as the two of them fell.

They landed at the bottom of the steps, and Maya heard the groan that came as the air was knocked out of Hewitt's lungs. Even so, he tried to fight her, grabbing for the arm that held the gun.

Maya knew that she couldn't let him get to it. Given what she suspected he'd done to Anne, she knew he wouldn't hesitate to turn her own weapon on her. Grappled together like this, retaining control of the Glock was everything.

Maya twisted the arm free, and elbowed Hewitt back with her free arm. He tried to grab onto her and pull her in, but she hit him with the butt of the gun then, sending him sprawling at the base of the steps.

Maya took two steps back up them, giving him no room in which to throw himself at her, even if he weren't busy groaning with pain. Maya had her own pain to ignore, in the form of something sharp and stabbing among her ribs where she'd struck the steps. Right then, though, she didn't care. The adrenaline pumping through her was more than enough to get her through the next part.

"Hewitt James," she said. "You are under arrest."

CHAPTER TWENTY SIX

Maya was getting frustrated again, because of the time it took to do everything. Time to get Hewitt James back to Cleveland, time to get him processed, time to find a public defender for him.

It didn't help that throughout all of it, he wasn't talking. He was just sitting there in an interview room on the other side of a sheet of one-way glass, staring back at it as if he knew that Maya and Marco were on the other side of it.

"He won't even let me get a step into the room before he says he wants his lawyer," Maya said.

"We've got him. We just have to be patient for this part," Marco said. "Just the fact that he's clamming up like this says he's worried about something."

"Or just that he's learned never to talk to the cops," Maya pointed out. "You say he's been in trouble all his life? Well, maybe he's learned that nothing good comes of talking."

"Columbus PD are tossing his house," Marco said. "They're not too happy about us going there without letting them know, but when I mentioned the FBI they agreed. If there's any link to Anne, they'll find it."

There was something about his confidence that was infectious, and for at least a moment or two, Maya started to feel good about all of this.

Then Hewitt's lawyer arrived.

"Why is my client in an interview room without me?" he demanded as he walked in. He was a short, slightly built man of about fifty, in a cheap suit and with a briefcase that looked as if it had been through far too much.

"You're the public defender?" Maya said. "Good, then we can finally get on with this."

"*After* I confer with my client about all the ways you've breached his rights. What's that bruising on his head? You attacked him?"

"*He* attempted to attack *me*," Maya said. "So we could add assault on an FBI Agent to the list of charges if you want, but I think murder will be more than enough."

"Murder?" the public defender said.

151

"The murder of Anne Postmartin," Maya said. "Haven't you even read the file?"

"I... I need to confer with my client," the lawyer said.

Maya waited for him to go into the interview room, waited for him to talk things over in low tones with Hewitt James. Legally, Maya couldn't listen in, but there was nothing to stop her from watching the expression on his face as his overworked, underprepared lawyer told him what this was about. Maya was expecting many things, from fear to denial, despair to anger.

She wasn't expecting relief.

Maya knew that she had to get in there then. She had to know what was going on. Not waiting for the public defender to finish, she stepped into the interview room with Marco following in her wake. She stepped over to its table and started the recorder so that they would miss anything.

"Agent," the lawyer said. "I wasn't finished."

"Why do you look so relieved, Hewitt?" Maya said. "What? You're glad that we finally caught up with you?"

She thought that Hewitt might not answer, but he shook his head.

"I'm just surprised that it took you all so long to find me. To figure it out."

"That you're Anne Postmartin's killer?" Maya said. She needed to hear the words. More than that, a confession would bring this to a clean end, something that the kidnapper wouldn't be able to argue with. It would be done, and Maya might get her sister back.

"That I was her *boyfriend*," Hewitt shot back, anger suddenly flickering across his face. He started to stand up, but his lawyer's hand on his arm stopped him. "I didn't kill her. You can't pin that on me."

Maya took a seat on the opposite side of the interview room's small table.

"Are you trying to tell us that you *didn't* kill her?" Marco asked, taking his own seat.

Maya caught the flash of indignation that crossed Hewitt's face.

"That's what I just said," Hewitt snapped back. "I didn't kill Anne. I *couldn't* kill Anne. I loved her!"

"You think every man who kills a woman he was in a relationship with doesn't say that?" Marco replied. "You think I haven't heard it from a dozen scumbags who talk about how much they love someone even while they've got her blood on their hands?"

"It wasn't me!" Hewitt said.

"Why were the two of you so secretive?" Maya asked, wanting to back down from the simple rounds of accusation and refusal.

"Why do you think?" Hewitt demanded. "Her parents. That dad of hers would never have accepted her seeing a guy like me. I couldn't even show up on her socials, because he was all over them, curating his precious daughter's online image."

It helped to explain why there was no trace of him in Anne's life beyond that yearbook.

"She kept you a very close secret," Maya said. "Didn't tell her friends, didn't tell her parents. Was she ashamed of you, Hewitt?"

"No, she wasn't 'ashamed' of me," Hewitt replied. Maya watched his reaction, but it was mostly the same honest anger that she'd gotten from the rest of this.

"Because it's easy to see how things could have gone," Maya said. "Maybe you did love Anne, and maybe you didn't like that she wouldn't tell anyone in her life about you. So you pushed for it, and you pushed for it, and she refused, and that made you angry."

"Are you asking a question, Agent?" the lawyer asked.

"Is that what happened, Hewitt?" Maya asked.

Hewitt was already shaking his head as she asked it. "No, that wasn't what happened. Anne didn't like the sneaking around any more than I did, but she was *committed* to me. She went to the same crappy college as me, when she could have been off in New York, or somewhere. We were saving all the money we could get. When we had enough, we were going to move in together and let everyone know. I was going to *marry* Anne."

"Maybe that was your plan," Marco said. "Maybe that was what happened that night. Maybe you met up with her and proposed in those woods, then when she said no, you strangled her."

"I wasn't even *there*, man!" Hewitt snapped, starting to stand.

"Sit down, Hewitt," Maya ordered him, and he did so, looking surprised at the steel in her tone. "If you weren't there, where were you?"

"I don't remember," Hewitt said. His hands twitched nervously as he did it.

"I don't believe you," Maya said. "You don't knoq where you were the night your girlfriend was murdered? You remember every second of that night. Anne went to that stand of trees after the show voluntarily. The only person she would go there to meet alone like that is *you*. You used to meet there, right? You arranged to meet her?"

"I…" Hewitt looked over to his lawyer, and for a moment or two, Maya thought that he might just say nothing. "Yes, all right. I arranged to meet her. Those trees near the shoreline were where we would meet up. We could do it without people seeing we were together."

"And you were going to meet up after the show," Maya said.

"We were," Hewitt admitted. "But I wasn't there."

"Then where were you?" Marco asked. He clearly didn't want to let this go either.

Maya watched as Hewitt held a brief, whispered conversation with his appointed lawyer. Finally, he answered.

"I was at a drug deal, ok?" Marco said. "I was meeting up with my boys, and couldn't exactly say 'wait until tomorrow while I see my girl' you know? So I was late. I was late, and…"

"And in that time, someone had killed Anne," Maya said.

She saw the look of pain that crossed Hewitt's face. He nodded. "I always came to the trees from the far side, over the rocks, so no one would see. She wasn't there when I got there. I thought… I thought she was angry with me because I was late. I thought I'd make it up to her the next day. Then I heard what had happened and…"

Hewitt put his head in his hands. Maya was pretty sure that he was crying.

"I couldn't even go to her funeral," Hewitt said. "Because no one knew I was her boyfriend."

"So these people you met for the drug deal," Marco said. "Who were they?"

"I don't know, man," Hewitt said. "Just some guys who needed some stuff."

Who they would probably never be able to find again, even if Hewitt was willing to give them their actual names. Even if he *knew* them.

"So you're saying you don't have a real alibi," Marco said.

"I didn't *do* this!" Hewitt insisted.

"Then why did you run, Hewitt?" Maya asked.

There was another whispered conversation with his lawyer. This time, it was the lawyer who answered.

"My client wishes to make it known that he fled in relation to his… other endeavors, not because of anything to do with the death of Anne Postmartin."

154

He'd run, in other words, because running was what you did when the police came to the door. Probably, Maya thought, the Columbia police would find whatever stash he was planning to sell on soon.

"Ok," Maya said. "That's enough for now. Hewitt, if there's anything you're leaving out, I strongly suggest that you tell us when we come back in."

Maya turned off the recorder and left with Marco. Outside, she found three or four of the precinct's detectives standing watching, including Chief Linden. He stood there for a moment or two, then actually burst into applause, echoed by a couple of the detectives there.

"Well done, Agent Gray. I'll admit that your methods had me worried, but it seems that you get results. You've actually done it. You've actually *caught* Anne Postmartin's killer. With assistance from our own department, of course."

Maya could see him lining up to take the credit already. Marco put a hand on Maya's shoulder.

"You've done it, Maya," he said. "You've got him."

There was only one problem with that: Maya didn't think Hewitt had done it. He was undoubtedly guilty of plenty of things, but Maya believed him. She believed that Hewitt had gone to those woods looking for Anne and missed her because she was already dead. She believed his anger, and his grief.

Maya wanted it to be true. She *wanted* Hewitt to be the killer, because that would close the case. That would beat the looming deadline and save a woman's life. Maybe her sister's life.

Even so, Maya didn't believe it was him.

Maya turned to tell Marco all of that, but there was no time, because that was when she saw the two people who should have been nowhere near the precinct walk in: Anne's parents.

"Where is he?" Jon Postmartin bellowed. "Where's the guy who killed my baby?"

He stormed forward towards the interview room as if he might burst in there and tear Hewitt apart with his bare hands.

"You can't go in there, Mr. Postmartin," Marco said, moving into his path.

"The hell I can't!" Jon bellowed, still trying to force his way forward. "This is the man who killed my daughter."

"We have to do it properly," Chief Linden said, as a couple of detectives moved to hold back Jon Postmartin. "He'll get what's

155

coming to him, but you have to let us do our jobs. He'll be charged, he'll be tried, and he'll get *everything* he deserves."

"I don't think it's him," Maya said, in the space that followed.

"What?" Chief Linden said. "Did you listen to your own interrogation, Agent? A lowlife with no alibi and every reason to kill Anne Postmartin? Of *course* it was him."

Maya still didn't believe it, though. "He loved Anne, and I don't think he was lying about what happened that night."

"Then you're fooling yourself," Chief Linden said. "We're holding Hewitt James, and we're charging him with murder. Case closed."

The only problem, as far as Maya was concerned, was that it seemed anything but that.

CHAPTER TWENTY SEVEN

Maya had to get out of there, because she couldn't stand the atmosphere of self-congratulation that was building up in the station. She stepped outside and was almost surprised to find that darkness had fallen. Between the forensics, the journey to Columbus and back, and the interrogation, she'd burnt up most of her last day on the case.

"Maya?" Marco said, following her out. "Are you serious about what you said in there? You don't think it's him?"

"I know I *should*," Maya said.

"Because all the evidence points that way," Marco pointed out. "Evidence *you* found."

"I know he doesn't have an alibi. I know he's all kinds of trouble."

"Not just that," Marco said. "You found the boyfriend angle. It makes *sense*, when none of the rest of it does. You said it was either a boyfriend or someone at the dance studio, and we've established that it *can't* be anyone at the dance studio."

"I know that too," Maya said. She leaned back against the wall of the station. After the days she'd spent working on this case, she felt tired.

"Sometimes, you've just got to take the win," Marco said.

Take the win.

Sometimes, Maya knew, that was what you had to do. It wasn't about what she felt in a case, but about what the evidence said. It was just that usually, there was more satisfaction than this when she reached the place that the evidence led.

Maya could hear the tiredness in Marco's voice. He'd been working as hard and as long as her on this. Longer, because he'd been the one who'd had to live with not solving the case for the last two years.

"I just don't believe he did it, Marco," Maya said.

"Everyone else does."

Maya looked him in the eye. "Do you?"

Maya could see him thinking it over. She could see how much he wanted to be over.

"I trust you," Marco said. "I've seen how you read people, and you've made more progress with this case in days than I managed in

157

two years. I *want* this to be over, but if you say it's not, then I'll go along with it."

That meant more to Maya than she could say. The relief of that flooded through her.

"I'm the only one who will, though," Marco said. "You heard Chief Linden back in there. They're holding Hewitt James for the murder. He's going to recommend charging him to the DA. He's probably organizing a party in there right now to celebrate closing the case."

"Because he played such a big part in it?"

"Whatever he did or didn't do, he'll be the one giving the press conference," Marco said. "My guess is that he's called at least half a dozen newspapers already. Which means that there will be no way he'll let you do anything else on this case."

"*Let* me?" Maya said.

"A single murder inside a state, with no serial killer. He claimed jurisdiction before, and he'll do it now."

"We'll see about that," Maya said, and got out her phone to call Harris.

It was getting late, but he still answered almost instantly.

"Gray, I thought I'd hear from you!" he said. He sounded excited, happy, which could mean only one thing.

"You heard about Hewitt James?" Maya said.

"I did. Chief Linden called me just a minute ago. Congratulations, Gray, you actually solved this!"

"It's more complicated than that, sir," Maya said.

She heard silence on the other end of the line.

"How *much* more complicated?" Harris asked. He didn't sound quite so happy anymore.

"I don't believe Hewitt James did this."

"Gray." *Really* unhappy now. "This is not the time to start joking."

"I'm not joking," Maya said. "I've talked to him, and I don't believe he did this."

"That's not enough, Gray," Harris said. "Chief Linden told me the case against him, and I agree it's enough to charge him. We're supporting that decision."

"But sir-" Maya began.

"No. Listen to me, Gray. You've said yourself that a woman's life depends on this, and there's no time left. We have enough of a case against this Hewitt James to charge him, and we're doing it. You've done good work. Do *not* mess it up now. Your sister's life could depend on it."

"That was a low blow," Maya said.

"I don't care," Harris replied. "This is done. Accept that, Gray. That's an order."

He hung up, leaving Maya standing there, feeling bereft. She'd pushed this as far as it was possible to push it, and still, no one seemed willing to believe her when she said that there was further to go.

"This is going to be a witch hunt," Maya said.

"What?" Marco replied.

"There's not going to be any physical evidence, but they'll go after Hewitt hard anyway, back themselves to convince a jury. Maybe they *will* be convinced, and he'll go away for the rest of his life. All to get a result."

"What's the alternative, Maya?" Marco asked. "We don't have much time left."

They didn't, but would all of this even be enough to convince the kidnapper? Would he settle for a trial without anything behind it other than a story that sounded plausible, a suspect with a bad record, and the lack of an alibi?

Could Maya really just let this go, when she was sure that she'd made a mistake? Could she send the wrong person to prison, even to save someone's life? Even for her sister?

"I have to talk to Hewitt James again," Maya said.

Marco was already shaking his head. "Linden will never allow it now. He'll be keeping him locked down as soon as he's out of the interview room."

"Which is why I need you to distract him for me," Maya said.

She thought that Marco might hesitate, that she might even have to talk him into it. What she was asking was a big deal, after all. It could even cost Marco his career.

"All right," Marco said, surprising her by saying it after only a second or two. "I can probably keep his attention, but not for long."

Maya nodded, and headed back into the building, determined to find out the truth.

Marco had been right about it being a party atmosphere in there. It looked as though someone had found a box of pastries, and someone else had dug out a bottle of scotch that probably wasn't supposed to be sitting at the bottom of a desk. Chief Linden was sitting in the middle of it all, looking happier than Maya had seen him since she'd been there. The detectives were crowded around him, basking in the moment that the case was closed, even though none of them had actually contributed to closing it.

Marco went over to it all, and suddenly *he* was the center of attention. Maya saw Chief Linden clap him on the back.

"So, tell us all how you did it," Chief Linden said. "I want to get the role our detectives played in never giving up on the Anne Postmartin case right for the press conference."

Marco's expression initially showed exactly how uncomfortable he was taking all the credit for the case. Then he caught Maya's eye, and Maya nodded to remind him what he was there to do.

"Well, I knew from the start that there was more to the case than just the Moonlight Killer, sir," Marco said. "But it was just a question of finding the right angle. Agent Gray and I-"

"Oh, we don't need to hear about Agent Gray," Chief Linden said. If it hadn't been clear before that he intended to grab the credit for this case before, then it was abundantly clear now. "I'm sure that your contribution was the crucial one."

Marco glanced across again, and Maya gave him another encouraging nod.

"I certainly knew that there was more to it. The whole boyfriend angle was crucial. From the moment we… I visited the scene I knew that Anne had to have gone there to meet with someone she trusted."

While Marco held the detectives' attention, Maya crept towards the interview suite. She could see Hewitt's lawyer in there with him, presumably wanting to talk him through everything that would happen next, and what their options were. Maya guessed that he might be having trouble finding any.

Maya knocked on the door and put her head around it.

"Chief Linden would like to speak to you," she said to the lawyer. "Something about the DA and a deal."

The lawyer leapt up. "Hewitt, I need to go see what this is about. Don't say anything to anyone while I'm gone."

He left, and even as he did so, Maya slipped into the room.

"I'm not saying anything to you," Hewitt said, crossing his arms pointedly as Maya sat down. "You heard the lawyer guy. Nothing."

Very carefully, Maya leaned forward and made sure that the recorders were off.

"There. Nothing you say now will be admissible. You could come out and tell me that you killed Anne and it still wouldn't count for anything in court."

"I *didn't* kill Anne!" Hewitt said. "I keep telling you."

Maya nodded. "I believe you."

He stopped short, staring at her like he couldn't quite understand it all. "Then what am I doing here?"

"Because right now, everyone else out there, *everyone*, is convinced that you did it. Even your own lawyer went rushing out at the sound of a deal because he thinks you're guilty, and he's just trying to find a way to make sure that you do as little time as possible."

That got another look of surprise, quickly mixed with suspicion. "No, this is some kind of trick. You're trying to get me to say something incriminating. I'll wait for my lawyer."

"Then don't talk," Maya said. "Just listen. Right now, you're looking at spending the rest of your life behind bars. I don't think you killed Anne, but just me saying that isn't going to convince anyone. Unless you give me something else, I can't help you."

"So what?" Hewitt said. "I'm supposed to prove that I'm innocent?"

"I need to find the *real* killer," Maya said. "But I can't do that without information. You were closer to Anne than anyone else. You must have known her as well as anyone by the time of her death. I need to know the things that other people don't know. The things that only you can tell me."

Hewitt looked down at his hands, not saying anything. The rest of the time, he'd been staring at her, but he chose *now* to look away?

"What is it, Hewitt? What do you know?" Maya said. "There's something, isn't there? Look at me."

He looked up at her, and Maya could see the strain in his face. There was something, Maya knew it.

"There's something, but I can't tell you. I had to promise never to tell anyone before she would tell me. She was so upset, but even then, she wouldn't tell me. Not until I swore I would never, ever tell anyone else."

Maya knew that she had to play this carefully, but she also knew that she didn't have much time. It would be only a matter of a few more seconds before the lawyer came bursting back in here, probably accompanied by half of the precinct, ready to throw her out.

"Anne is gone, Hewitt," Maya said. "Whatever it is, it can't hurt her anymore. But keeping this secret can hurt you. Anne loved you? Well, she wouldn't want to see you go to jail for something you didn't do. She wouldn't want you to go to prison just for keeping her secrets."

Maya saw Hewitt swallow, obviously considering it.

"All right," he said, giving in at last. "I... I'll tell you what I know."

CHAPTER TWENTY EIGHT

Maya was just opening the door to the interview room again when Hewitt's lawyer came running to it, accompanied by Chief Linden.

"What are you doing in here, Agent?" the lawyer said. "Anything that my client has said without me present will be completely inadmissible."

"If you've jeopardized this case, Gray, I'll see that your bosses hear exactly how you let a killer go free!"

"It's all right," Maya said. "I'm going."

"Yes, you are," Linden said. "Get out of my station. Get *out* of my precinct and don't come back."

Maya didn't even dignify that with a response. She walked past him instead, checking an address on her phone as she went. She reached Marco, putting a hand on his arm to pull him out of the knot of detectives he was distracting and lowering her voice.

"I need you to come with me, right now."

Marco took one look at her expression and nodded. "All right. You've got something?"

"I've got something," Maya said.

"Where are we going?" Marco asked.

Maya held out her hand. "You'll see when we get there. I'll drive."

That took a second longer for Marco to give than the rest of it.

"I won't hurt your precious car," Maya promised, "but I'm driving."

Marco took out his keys and dropped them into her hand. She hurried out to the Explorer with him, all too aware that they didn't have much time left. Getting into the driver's seat, she set off through the streets of Cleveland.

"You're really not going to tell me where we're going?" Marco said.

Maya gestured to the GPS, where the address was clearly visible.

"Yes," Marco said. "But what's *there*, Maya?"

"You'll see," Maya replied, keeping her attention on the road. She didn't want to tell Marco before they got there, because she didn't want to give him a chance to talk her out of this.

They pulled up outside a mid-sized house in the suburbs, with a neatly kept lawn and a small sports car in the driveway. Maya headed up to the door with Marco following in her wake, and she ignored the doorbell, pounding on the door with her fist instead.

She waited in front of it impatiently. At least she was fairly sure *this* suspect wasn't going to run.

Finally, the door opened, revealing the face of the man she'd come to see.

"What are *you* doing here?" Lucas McFadden demanded. Maya could see the anger on his face as he saw her, the kind of indignation that she now realized was because he'd had something to hide. "You have no business being here!"

"I have one very important piece of business," Maya said. Beside her, she could see Marco's face. He looked surprised to see McFadden, but at least he wasn't trying to get in the way.

"Are you stupid, or just crazy?" McFadden said. "When my friend the mayor hears about this-"

"I don't think you're going to have many friends when this is done," Maya said. "Lucas McFadden, you're under arrest."

"What? You can't do this!" McFadden said. "FBI or not, I'll have your badge for this!"

"Marco, would you say that Mr. McFadden is resisting arrest?" Maya asked.

"I suppose so. but-"

Maya didn't wait for him to finish, because he didn't understand what was going on here. Instead, she stepped forward and hit Lucas McFadden, as hard and as sweetly as she could. It was a good punch. It connected perfectly with McFadden's jaw and he went down in a heap, just inside his front door.

He groaned and started to get up, but Maya was on him in an instant, half hoping that he would struggle so that she would have an excuse to hit him again. He seemed too stunned to do that, though, so she was able to roll him onto his stomach and get cuffs on him with relative ease.

"Maya?" Marco said. "What is all this about? What did Hewitt James *say* to you?"

Maya glared down at McFadden. "That's simple. You know how we thought there was something off about the dance studio? We were right. Lucas McFadden, you are under arrest for the sexual molestation of several minors, including Anne Postmartin."

164

They dragged McFadden back to the Explorer and threw him in the back, still cuffed. Marco drove, leaving Maya to sit in the passenger seat, feeling satisfied that at least they were getting this bastard behind bars.

"You can't do this!" McFadden insisted. "My friends-"

"How many friends do you think you'll have when what you did to those girls comes out?" Maya asked. "You say you've taught the mayor's daughter? What else did you do to her?"

"It wasn't like that!" McFadden insisted, as if he might explain it all, even now.

"So he killed Anne?" Marco said, with a glance back at the dance coach. "What was it, McFadden? She was going to tell people about what you'd done to her? She was going to come out and tell everyone when she had the platform of the nationals? So you had to kill her before she got there?"

"I didn't kill her!" McFadden said. "I wasn't anywhere near her that night! She'd been avoiding me for weeks, skipping private sessions because-"

"Because you were touching her inappropriately," Marco snapped. "That's what you were doing, wasn't it, McFadden?"

"Yes!" he said. "I'll admit that. I'll admit all of it, but not to killing Anne. Never that. She was my prize student, a *special* student."

He was breaking down now, starting to cry as they drove him back towards the precinct, as if that might get him some sympathy, rather than the disgust that filled Maya when she looked at him now. Just the thought of what he'd done to those girls made her want to pull the car over, take out her sidearm, and fill him full of bullets, but he was treating it as if it were some kind of *excuse*.

"Anne was so special that you just *had* to touch her?" Marco said, sounding just as disgusted as Maya felt.

"They were all special," McFadden managed, in between his tears. "Every one of them. I never *meant* for it to happen but working with someone in dance always builds such a strong bond, and they always looked so beautiful, so *elegant*. And they wanted it. I knew they wanted it."

Maya wanted nothing more than to hit him again, then.

"But then Anne didn't want it, and you killed her," Marco insisted.

165

"I didn't kill anyone!" McFadden said. "You've heard my alibi."

That was the problem. Maya had been through every second of that night through the witness statements, and McFadden simply hadn't had a chance to kill Anne. He was a monster, but not the one who had killed her.

"I only touched the special ones," McFadden said. He was more or less babbling now. "The best, the ones who made it to the troupe, who did extra work with me. Those were the only ones I could form that kind of connection with."

"The only ones you could scare into keeping your secret, you mean?" Marco snapped.

He had a point.

"We talked to all the girls in your troupe," Maya said. "Not one of them was willing to talk to us then, but I bet they will now. Do you know the damage you've done to them?"

"Damage?" McFadden said. "I helped to make them into great dancers. They were the special ones, the best. Do you know how many people tried out for my troupe and couldn't make it?"

"I'm sure you made them feel *very* special," Marco snapped back.

"Everybody shut up!" Maya said. Something caught at the edges of her mind. Something that wouldn't let go. "Marco, stop the car. I need to think."

Marco brought the Explorer to a halt, and Maya silently replayed the conversation in her head. Special. His troupe. The ones who made it.

"What about the ones who *didn't* make it?" Maya said. "Petronella gave us a list of the troupe, but what about the rest? Was there anyone who tried out and didn't make it who would be jealous of Anne? Anyone who couldn't take being rejected? You kept records, right?"

"I... I did," McFadden said, all the defiance gone from him now. "I keep them at the studio. If you take me there, I can get them.

*

They drove to the studio, where McFadden gave them access to his files on former students.

"Call a squad car," Maya said to Marco. "Get McFadden picked up. Unless you think Chief Linden is going to let him go?"

Marco shook his head. "Once he hears what McFadden did, he'll want him behind bars as badly as we do."

166

That was good enough for Maya, and it left her and Marco free to start looking through the files McFadden had amassed.

Where the list Petronella had given them was just names, every computer file was almost a complete biography of the would-be students, with details on the kids, their interests, who they were.

Almost as if McFadden had been looking for those students that he could pick out to keep a secret. No wonder he hadn't wanted her or Marco to have any access to them. The more Maya saw, the more grateful she was that the dance coach was going away.

There were details on the dancers' parents, too, with notes about who they were and what their connections were like. McFadden had liked to boast about who he knew, and it appeared that he hadn't left that to chance.

"It's like he was trying to psychologically profile them," Maya said.

"Does that mean *you* can?" Marco asked.

"I hope so."

If she could just find that one record…

Which, though? How could she narrow them down? No, she *could* do this. She just had to think.

Ok, so assume it was more likely to be a boy, but even that couldn't be certain. What else?

Someone who thought they should be there? Did that mean someone who was a good dancer?

Or just someone who was so used to succeeding that they couldn't?

Maya looked at one file, then another, trying to assess each student, trying to work out if they could have had a reason to kill Anne. It was uncomfortably close to the way McFadden had probably gone through these files looking for victims.

"It's taking too long," Maya said, looking through them.

It was getting close to midnight. Too close for comfort.

"You can do this, Maya," Marco assured her.

Would it have been better if they'd just stuck with Hewitt James? Would the kidnapper have accepted him as the killer? Would he *still* do so?

Then Maya saw a profile that caught her eye. It was for a young man named Kyle Brocker, and the moment Maya read through it, she found her eyes catching on it. Everything about this boy said accomplishment, drive, need to succeed. He'd been there at the same time as Anne, but crucially, he hadn't made the troupe. There was a

167

note about him shouting threats as he left. She looked at the date he'd tried out...

Maya knew that she had to go through the rest of the records, but even working through them quickly made it clear: none of them even came close.

Maya looked at her watch. One minute past midnight.

She was pretty sure that she'd found the killer, but she'd done it a minute too late. She'd missed the deadline, and now...

Had she failed? Was a woman going to die because of her?

CHAPTER TWENTY NINE

The good thing about the files from the dance studio was that they made it easy to find an address. They had to drive out to Hunting Valley, in the east of the city, and even by night, Maya could see that it was a seriously wealthy neighborhood.

Every house was a miniature mansion. Every driveway had an expensive sportscar or SUV on it. Maya guessed that it was *not* the kind of place used to police cars coming in with their lights flashing to clear the traffic in front of them.

She and Marco did so now, because there simply wasn't enough time to go any slower. They came skidding up the drive of the house they wanted, and Maya leapt out almost before they'd stopped. She ran up to the door and hammered on it.

It was a good couple of minutes before a young man answered, looking bleary eyed. Maya guessed that he'd just thrown on the jeans and shirt that he wore, because he was still barefoot. He was taller than her, close to Marco's height, and good looking in a clean cut, preppy kind of way.

"What's happening?" he said. "Do you know what time it is?"

"Probably better than you do," Maya said, because she could feel the seconds ticking away, each one screaming at her that the deadline was past, and a woman's life hung in the balance. "Kyle?"

"That's right, and you are?"

"Agent Gray, FBI. This is Detective Spinelli with the Cleveland PD. We need to ask a couple of questions. May we come in?"

"Now? All right. Come through."

He led the way through to a kitchen, where he put on coffee, obviously trying to wake up a little more while he answered questions.

"What did you want to ask me?" Kyle asked.

"Just one question," Maya said. "Why did you murder Anne Postmartin?"

He reeled from that question so badly that he almost knocked over the coffee maker.

"What? That's ridiculous!" Kyle said.

"I spent time before looking for any member of Lucas McFadden's troupe who might be jealous enough towards Anne to hurt her," Maya said. "But I forgot about people who didn't *make* the troupe. Like you. You tried out for the McFadden dance school's troupe two days before Anne's death, right?"

"I mean, I did, but this... you think I killed her?"

Maya nodded. She could see the way Kyle was looking round, hunting for an exit, like he was about to make a run for it. She could *see* the guilt etched into his features.

"I think you were jealous," Maya said. "I bet, when I talk to the members of the troupe, they'll remember. You're a good-looking guy, they'd have noticed you. They would have seen when you failed to make the grade."

Maya saw a little twitch as she said 'failed.'

"You were humiliated, weren't you?" Maya insisted. "Did they laugh at you? I bet McFadden did. I bet the girls in his troupe did too, because they were all so afraid of him that they would have laughed along, and let's face it, because teenage girls can be cruel."

"This is nonsense," Kyle said.

"Is this not what happened?" Maya asked. She wanted to keep him on the back foot with this, to keep the pressure going. It was her only chance to get him to crack. "You were so jealous of them, and Anne was the natural target for that jealousy, because she was the best performer there. She was the one who was going to the nationals. She was the one who was front and center on the stage. So you killed her."

"Of course I didn't kill her," Kyle said, but there was a slight hesitation before he said it, as though he had to take the time to marshal his responses. Maya could *feel* the lies there.

"You watched her," Maya said. "I bet if we go back through footage from the days around her death, we'll see you lurking in the background. No one would have paid attention to you before, but we will now."

"This..." Kyle started to back away, but Marco moved to intercept him.

"Better if you stay there," Marco said.

"You saw where Anne met her boyfriend," Maya said. "Or maybe you just followed her on the night of the show. You took gloves with you to make sure that you wouldn't leave physical evidence. That's premeditation, Kyle."

"Premeditation of what?" Kyle snapped. "I didn't do anything."

170

But he wasn't convincing. Maya had heard denials from other people in this case, and there had been a genuine outrage at being accused. With Kyle, all she saw were flickers of fear and guilt.

"You strangled Anne Postmartin," Maya said. "You dragged her body down to the lake. And then, what was it, Kyle? Did someone nearly spot you? Did you just get tired of dragging her? Or did you look up, see the moon, and realize that people might blame the Moonlight Killer?"

Kyle was silent for a second or two, and for a moment, Maya thought that she'd broken through. Her only hope was to shock him into a confession with the suddenness of the accusations, and for a moment, she thought that she had him.

Then he laughed. He laughed in her face.

"Are you kidding with all this?" he asked. "You know I'm going to law school now, right? Can you prove any of this? You say the killer, whoever he was, wore gloves? So do you have any physical evidence? Do you have any witnesses?"

"We'll find some," Maya said.

"Oh, yeah, you said. You'll go back through the footage, and find me watching Anne Postmartin? Even if there *were* that kind of footage out there, what would it prove? You've got nothing and you know it."

You've got nothing. He wasn't saying that he hadn't done it anymore; instead, he was simply saying that he was going to get away with it, because they couldn't prove any of it.

The worst part of it was that he was right.

Maya had no proof.

"Do you have an alibi for that night?" Marco asked. It was a good question, a sensible question.

"I went to see the show down on the beach," Kyle said.

"So you admit that you were there?" Maya asked. He was willing to give them that much?

"Of course. I'm sure that if you look for witnesses, you'll find plenty who remember me. I'm told that I'm pretty memorable."

Was that him throwing Maya's own words back in her face?

"Of course, that doesn't matter," Kyle said. "Plenty of other people were. Are you going to go round to all of their houses after midnight, accusing *them*?"

Again, this wasn't the indignation that she'd had from the others. This was a kind of cockiness, even arrogance, there. He was *enjoying* this now. He was enjoying winning this, being better than them.

171

"Not when I have the killer standing right in front of me," Maya said. "It's you, Kyle. I know it's you."

"Then *prove* it," Kyle replied, with the certainty of someone who believed that they were in the clear.

"You think you've won this, don't you?" Marco said, and there was a restlessness in him, like he wanted to act, like he wanted to move. Like he wanted to hit Kyle until he confessed. "You like winning, Kyle?"

"I find it's a lot better than losing," Kyle replied.

"Yes, I saw that, when Maya showed me your file," Marco said. "You see, I know kids like you, from around here. Want to be the best at everything, and usually, you succeed. Not that you have to try for it. How much of that success did your parents buy for you?"

"I achieved everything I have without anyone's help!" Kyle snapped back, and there was a note of real anger there in a way there hadn't been when Maya had accused him of murder.

She realized what Marco was doing. He'd found the one weakness a young man like this might have. He had to be perfect, and people had to *know* that he was perfect.

"You know that Lucas McFadden kept files on his students?" Maya said. "They told me a lot about you. You were valedictorian of your class, but then, I imagine your parents paid for better tutors than anyone else got. You were on the basketball team, but who wouldn't want the popular guy on the team?"

"I know what you're doing," Kyle said, but he still didn't look happy about it.

"It said you were a soloist in the church choir," Maya said. "Everything you've decided you wanted, you got. How big a donation did your parents make to the church?"

"*I* did all of that!" Kyle snapped. "Not them, me!"

"You say you're in law school now," Maya said. "What is it, getting ready to be a VP in daddy's business?"

"I'm doing that myself!" Kyle insisted, in an even angrier tone.

"But why here, Kyle?" Maya asked. "Why aren't you off at Harvard or Princeton? That's the kind of school that a kid like you should be able to buy your way into, right?"

"You bitch, I'll-"

"You'll what?" Maya said. "Strangle me?"

She could see that Kyle was sweating now. He'd looked so comfortable for the rest of this, but now, suddenly, he looked as if he would rather be anywhere else.

"I think you hate that you keep achieving things, but it never feels like it's quite your own achievement," Maya said. "I bet that you even hate this house, because it's paid for out of your trust fund, or it's technically owned by one of your father's businesses, right Kyle?"

He didn't even answer that one. Maya could feel him there on the edge. He was so close to snapping. She had to believe that, because if she couldn't get him to do that much, then she really *didn't* have a case, and all the work of the last few days, all the effort, would have been for nothing.

In that moment, Maya realized that she understood this young man better than she thought, better than she wanted to.

"There's nothing like putting in the work to achieve something and then seeing it go right," Maya said. "It can be hard, making an effort, trying to get things to turn out the way you want, but when they do, it feels better than anything else."

The way it did when she closed a case. Suddenly, all the work she'd put in seemed worth it.

"But you… you could never be sure if it was your work making everything happen," Maya said. "Your parents were always there, helping, making things easier. You wanted something where you could succeed on your own terms. Was dance a secret passion for you, Kyle? Something you didn't share with your parents?"

"Something you *deliberately* didn't share?" Marco said, backing Maya up.

Maya nodded. "You wanted it to be your thing. Your own success. And you *had* to succeed. So you went to the McFadden dance school and you tried out. You assumed you'd be praised, applauded, but you were ridiculed. The only thing you've ever done for yourself, and you failed at it. You were a failure, Kyle, and you couldn't stand it."

"No, it wasn't like that!" he said. "I was the best!"

"*Anne* was the best," Maya said. "And you killed her for it."

Even now, they didn't have the confession they needed. They didn't have evidence. All Kyle had to do was keep quiet, and he could get away with murder. Maya could see him sweating, though. He was too rattled now. He-

He shoved Marco, breaking away from him, and then set off running, out of the back door of the house and into the yard.

CHAPTER THIRTY

Maya set off in pursuit as soon as Kyle ran, sprinting out of the kitchen and following him into the yard beyond. He threw off the contents of the kitchen counter into her path, but Maya dodged them, keeping up the chase even as the coffeemaker shattered on the floor.

She burst through the back door of the house, into a large yard, complete with a pool. Kyle's bare feet slapped on the wet tiles, and Maya followed him round it, determined to bring him down as quickly as possible. She didn't have *time* for some long chase.

The good news was that Kyle wasn't as used to trying to run as Hewitt James had been. Hewitt would already have been out of the yard, but Kyle was still making his way around the pool, shoving a couple of lawn chairs into her path.

Maya hurdled them, then put on a burst of speed and tackled Kyle. The young man was bigger than her, but Maya had momentum on her side, and she went low, catching him around the knees.

They both tumbled back, into the pool.

The water hit Maya in a shock of cold, and for a moment, both she and Kyle went under. She at least had the advantage that she'd been expecting the plunge into the pool. Kyle was spluttering and flailing as they both went under the water.

He kicked out at her, but the water robbed the movement of any impact. Maya grabbed the leg and pulled him closer, clambering over him towards the surface. Kyle grabbed her in return, each of them struggling to come out on top.

Maya hit him, and even though there wasn't as much impact in the water, she managed to get him to gasp, knocking some of the air out of him. Maya saw a brief look of fury cross Kyle's face, and then he reached out his hands for her throat.

They fastened around her neck with crushing force, and for a second or two, Maya understood what it must have been like for Anne Postmartin in the moments before her death. There was the rushing pressure as the blood flow to her brain cut off, the sense of the world closing in, and the fear that maybe this *would* be the end for her.

But she wasn't a helpless young dancer. She wasn't another victim Kyle could choke the life from. Stiffening her fingers, Maya drove them into the front of Kyle's throat, driving him back and breaking the grip as he gagged.

She drove up towards the surface and broke through it before Kyle did. Maya grabbed him, holding him under a second or two longer, then yanked him up, spluttering.

"Admit it!" she yelled in his face. "Admit what you did!"

She plunged him down under the water again as he tried to fight clear of her holding him there until the fight started to go out of him. Maya dragged him up again.

"Admit it!"

"She was so perfect..." Kyle said, "...and when they all laughed at me, I couldn't stand it! Why should she get to be that good, when *I* failed?"

Maya dragged him over to the side of the pool, where Marco helped them out. Maya slapped cuffs on Kyle, but Marco was the one to read him his rights. This was his city, and a case he'd been working for years. It seemed only right to give him that much.

Now that he'd started talking, Kyle didn't seem inclined to stop.

"Do you know what it's like with that pressure to be the best at everything?" he demanded. "But never knowing if it's really you? Then the one thing I try on my own, I fail at? I *had* to kill her. This has ruined my life!"

Maya wasn't listening now. It was enough that he was admitting what he'd done. Her attention was more on the time. Almost one AM. Well past the deadline, but there was nothing she could do to change that.

They dragged Kyle back to the car. Maya didn't care that the two of them were still soaked from their plunge into the pool. That didn't matter. What mattered was that they needed to get Kyle back to the station, declare an end to this, and *hope* that it would be enough to satisfy the kidnapper.

How would he know? That was the question. It was obvious that he was monitoring things somehow, but how? Guessing that he might monitor the police radios via a scanner, Maya called it in. It was her best, only, hope of bringing this to an end.

"This is Agent Gray of the FBI. We've caught Anne Postmartin's killer. Her *real* killer."

CHAPTER THIRTY ONE

They drove back to the station, and even as they walked through the doors, Chief Linden was waiting for them. Maya could see the anger on his face.

"You've gone too far this time, Agent," he said.

"By finding Anne's actual killer?" Maya asked. She'd had enough of the police chief, and now that the case was done, she didn't see any reason to hold back. "By arresting a child molester you insisted was an upstanding citizen? Or by ruining your press conference?"

He looked as if he might boil over. "We *have* Anne Postmartin's killer. What is this, and who is this young man?"

"This is Kyle Brocker," Maya said. "Anne Postmartin's murderer. Isn't that right, Kyle?"

Beside her, Kyle was still soaked to the skin from going into the pool, and Maya was pretty sure that there were more than a few of his own tears mixed in with the rest of the moisture. Even so, he nodded.

"I did it," he said.

Maya saw the expression on Chief Linden's face shift, first to something like shock, then to a more thoughtful kind of expression as he tried to work out what was going on. He still looked angry, but at least it was a kind of angry that wasn't going to get in the way of him actually doing his job.

"All right," he said. "Book him and get him into an interview room. But neither of you are going anywhere near it. I want to hear this for myself."

Maya should probably have argued about having the interrogation taken away from her, but right then, she didn't care if it meant that they got the confession down on tape.

"Be quick and you can probably still give your press conference," Maya said. She was too tired to care about Chief Linden anymore. Instead, she took Kyle through to an interview room, then looked back towards the office that she and Marco had shared throughout all this.

Marco obviously caught her glance.

"Oh no," he said. "One night of you falling asleep in an office chair is enough. I'll drive you back to your hotel. You probably need to get out of those wet clothes."

"Is that an offer, Detective?" Maya asked. She was too tired to actually make good on the flirting, but it felt good to be able to do it.

"Maybe when you're not about to fall over from running around all day and all night," Marco said.

"I can keep up with you anytime," Maya said.

"I believe you," Marco replied. He stopped in front of her. "I just want to say thank you. This has been two years of my life, Gray, and you actually solved it. Whatever happens now, remember that you're still the one who found Anne's killer."

Maya knew that was a big deal. Ordinarily, she would have felt the overwhelming satisfaction of a job well done. Now though, she couldn't stop worrying. Would it be enough, or had it all been for nothing? She found herself going back over every false turn they'd taken in the case, every hour wasted.

Had one of those cost Liza Carty her life?

*

Maya hadn't slept all night, monitoring her phone with one eye open, hoping for a call, a text, some indicator that the girl would be set loose.

But nothing came.

The sun had barely broken over the horizon when a knocking came on her door. She jumped out and yanked it open to see Marco standing there.

"Anything?" she asked hopefully.

He shook his head.

He handed her a cup of coffee.

"You look like you can use this," he said. "You didn't sleep, did you?"

Maya shook her head, took it gratefully, and gulped it down.

He held out a doughnut.

She ate it hungrily.

"What would I do without you?" Maya said.

"I called in briefly before I came here," Marco said, stepping into the room while Maya got her things together. "Kyle Brocker has given a full confession, right down to how he tried to make the whole thing look like the Moonlight Killer so that he could get away with it."

Maya sighed with relief. It was frustrating being shut out of the interview room, but if it meant they'd gotten the right result, then it didn't matter.

"And Chief Linden is still pissed at me?" Maya said.

Marco shrugged. "Let's just say that he's happy now that the case is closed, because you have no reason to stick around."

"And you?" Maya asked, before she could stop herself.

"I'm happy the case is closed," Marco said. "I'm happy we got justice for Anne. The part where you aren't sticking around? That's more of a pity."

It felt like a pity from Maya's side too. With the case going on, there had never been a chance for anything to happen with her and Marco, and now she would be going back to DC, hours away. It looked as though it was just not meant to be.

"Chief Linden will have to see me at least one more time," Maya said. "I'll need to go in, wrap up the loose ends. I should call Deputy Director Harris, too."

That was the thing with a case: finding the answer was never quite the end. They always needed to build the evidence, to go through the process of the trial. Probably, Maya would have to testify.

She was still thinking about all that when she saw the rectangle of cardboard on the floor near Marco's feet.

Maya's heart leapt into her mouth. Another postcard? Here? Fear filled her at the sight of it, because she could imagine all too easily what it might contain: details of where to find Liza Carty's body, maybe even a picture of her dead. This could oh so easily be the kidnapper telling her that she'd lost his little game.

But she also allowed herself a tinge of hope. Maybe, just maybe, she was still alive.

There was no clue from the front of the postcard as to what it might contain, just another picture of bunny rabbits hopping around a field. Maya lifted it, showing it to Marco.

"He got something *here*?" Marco said. "What does it say, Maya?"

Maya had to steel herself to read it, still certain that she might find herself reading the worst details of a woman's murder.

"Dear Maya," she read to Marco, "Congratulations on your arrest."

"You were right, he was listening in," Marco said.

Maya nodded. "Looks like it. There's more. 'Since this is your first attempt at playing our little game, and since you have pleased me by uncovering the truth when all around you wanted a lie, I have decided to allow a small grace period. Do not think that it will apply to our next endeavor together.'"

"The woman he took is still alive?" Marco asked.

Maya kept reading. "Liza Carty will be released at the coordinates at the bottom of this postcard at noon today. Do not attempt to capture me during the release, or she will die. Enjoy your success, Maya, because I will have another task for you to complete soon."

Maya swallowed at the threat of being made to go through all this again, but her sense of relief was greater. She'd actually managed to save one of the women this man was holding. A woman who might be able to tell her more, and who might even let her catch the kidnapper before he could hurt Megan.

She just had to get to the coordinates on the postcard by noon.

CHAPTER THIRTY TWO

Maya clung on in the Explorer as she and Marco raced to the location of the handover. They were entering a broad expanse of woodland now, going along what seemed to be an unpaved logging road, relying on the Explorer's navigation systems to get them where they needed to go.

"The FBI are meeting us at the drop off point, right?" Marco said.

Maya nodded. She didn't like having to bring in the others for this, but it would be stupid to go to such an isolated location without some kind of backup.

"Harris is arranging it," Maya said. The murder of Anne Postmartin had been a matter for the Cleveland PD, but this part was an FBI operation. She just hoped that after the business at the abandoned apartment building, he could still *get* her backup.

It turned out that he could. As Maya approached the drop off point, she and Marco found themselves flagged down by an agent in full tactical gear. Maya produced her ID, and as soon as she did, he waved the two of them off the road, onto a sidetrack. There, Maya saw a trio of vans, an ambulance, and at least a dozen armed agents. One addition told her just how seriously they were taking this:

Harris was there.

He was senior enough that he should have been behind his desk, dealing with everything else that came through the department even on a day like today. That he was out there said just how important this was to him.

Maya and Marco pulled up, and Harris was there waiting for them when they got out.

"Gray, well done on the case. Who is this?"

"Detective Spinelli of the Cleveland PD," Maya said. "He worked the case with me."

"Good enough," Harris said, and held out a hand for Marco to shake. "You said the handoff was due at noon?"

"Yes, sir," Maya said. She checked her watch. They still had most of an hour. "What's the set up here?"

"Follow me and I'll show you," Harris said. He led the way to one of the vans.

Inside, Maya saw a full tactical center set up, with screens for feeds from cameras they'd obviously set up around the area. A technician was monitoring them, along with what appeared to be a satellite view, complete with thermal imaging.

"We've established a perimeter," Harris said, "and we're using cameras to monitor anything that comes into it." He gestured to one of the screens, where Maya could see a broad clearing. "This is the place where the handover is due to happen."

"It's very open," Maya said. Why would the kidnapper choose such an open spot, with no cover to run to, in which to make the handover?

"Our guess is that he wants clear lines of sight," Harris said. "Or he's planning to hang back on the edge of the trees and send Liza Carty forward."

"Which is why you have the thermal imaging," Marco said.

Maya saw Harris nod.

"Not just that. We have agents spreading out, along with specialist snipers in ghillie suits. There's no way this guy could get within a mile of this spot, and we don't know about it. Once we know about it, there's no way he gets away. This ends today."

Harris sounded determined, but after the way things had happened at the apartment building, Maya was more cautious.

"He might not react well to another attempt to catch him," she said.

"Are you saying that we should all back off and leave you out there with him?" Harris replied. "Because that is *not* going to happen, Gray. We jumped through his hoops this time, but that's no guarantee of the safety of any of the other women. The only way this ends is if we catch him."

"I'm just saying that if we're doing this, it has to succeed," Maya said. She didn't mention the apartment building, but everything that had happened there seemed to hang in the air between them.

"This isn't the same," Harris said. "We control this situation, and he *has* to show. If he doesn't, he has no further leverage."

Except for the part where he still held twelve women, including her sister. Maya knew what he meant, though. The kidnapper could only get her to do anything while she believed that she might get Megan back for it. If he reneged, then he couldn't get anything more from her.

"You're going to be the one who meets Liza Carty and our kidnapper," Harris said. "Your job is to get him to come forward with

181

her into the open ground, preferably to get Ms. Carty away from him. After that, we take him."

Maya nodded. "Alive, though. We need him alive."

She needed him to tell her where her sister was, not for a sniper to put a bullet through him.

"If we can," Harris said. He reached down, taking a flak jacket from under one of the consoles in the van and passing it to Maya. "Put this on."

"It doesn't exactly show trust," Maya pointed out.

"I don't care about trust," Harris said. "I *do* care about the possibility that he might decide to kill you now that he's made you play his little game."

Maya didn't think that was likely, but she also knew there was no point in arguing with her boss. She took an earpiece for the same reason.

All there was to do now was wait and watch as the FBI tactical teams spread out, getting into position to cover the clearing.

"Movement," the technician said, and Maya felt her excitement building.

She checked her watch, ten minutes to twelve. If this was the kidnapper, he was early.

She jumped out of the van, and Marco went with her. Clearly he shared some of Harris's concerns, or he just wanted to be here for the finish of this. Together, they headed into the clearing.

"We have a figure approaching," Harris said, through Maya's earpiece. "Everyone stand ready. Only go on my signal."

Maya stood waiting, but she was worried now. Was Harris right? Was this the kidnapper approaching alone, getting into a position where he could pick her off? Had all of this been about getting her to do this one thing for him, and now it was done, he wanted her gone?

Maya's hand rested lightly on her gun, ready to draw it as soon as she saw any threat.

"Approaching figure is not the suspect, repeat, not the suspect," Harris said.

Even as he said it, a figure stumbled into the clearing: a young woman who was barefoot, dressed in what appeared to be a clean plastic evidence suit. As soon as she saw her, Maya started towards her, because she'd seen the features that stared at her in hope before. She knew them from the missing persons photograph she'd pulled up.

Liza Carty was there, and free.

"It's Liza," Maya said, touching her earpiece.

"Where's the kidnapper?" Harris demanded. "Somebody find me eyes on the kidnapper."

Maya ignored that, figuring that there were more than enough agents for the chase. Instead, she ran to Liza, and managed to get there just in time, as the young woman's legs gave out. She and Marco held her up between them.

"Liza, are you all right?" she asked. "I'm Agent Gray."

"Maya," Liza said, tears starting to fall from her eyes. "He called you Maya."

"The man who took you captive?" Maya said. "Is he here, Liza? Is he nearby?"

Liza shook her head. "He took me out of the place where he keeps the women. He put a blindfold on me and drove me somewhere. He took me out, told me to count to a thousand and then to walk straight towards the sun until I hit a big clearing. I've been walking so far."

Maya could see the cuts and scrapes on her feet. She must have been walking for miles.

"Harris," she said, touching her earpiece. "Stand down. The kidnapper isn't within your perimeter. He never was."

With that done, she turned her attention to Liza Carty.

"Come on, Liza," she said. "Let's get you somewhere safe."

She and Marco started to walk with Liza back in the direction of the waiting ambulance. It meant that they more or less had to carry her.

"You're safe now," Maya promised her. "No one else can hurt you."

And with that, Liza Carty passed out into Maya's arms.

CHAPTER THIRTY THREE

Maya sat in the ER with Marco, waiting for Liza Carty to wake up. She wasn't the only one. Currently, the ER had more FBI in it than it would have if there had been a terrorist threat.

Not that any of them could do anything. Currently, Liza was sedated in a room of her own while the doctors looked over her injuries and gave her a chance to recover. It meant a lot of waiting, but Maya would stay there as long as it took.

"When this done," Marco said, "stay in touch, ok? I want to know how the rest of this goes. If I can help, I will."

"And that's the only reason you want my number?" Maya said, trying to keep things light, but this wasn't a light moment.

"I'm serious, Maya," Marco said. "Anything you need, I'll be there. I know how important all this is."

That meant so much to her. As much as Maya tried to tell herself that she didn't need anyone, it definitely helped to know that she had someone who would be there if she ever did.

Even so, all they could do now was wait, trying to get to the point where Liza could give them some kind of answers. Maya sat there, trying to just switch off and wait, but unable to keep her mind from going back to thoughts of her sister, trapped there with Liza somewhere. Even if Liza could give her confirmation that Megan was alive, that would be something.

Maya hadn't realized just how much she'd drifted apart from her sister until some monster had kidnapped her. Now, she would do anything to get her back. Liza Carty lay sleeping in the next room, traumatized, but alive.

And for the first time in a long while, Maya dared to hope that maybe, just maybe, her sister was, too.

NOW AVAILABLE!

GIRL TWO: TAKEN
(A Maya Gray FBI Suspense Thriller —Book 2)

12 cold cases. 12 kidnapped women. One diabolical serial killer. In this riveting suspense thriller, a brilliant FBI agent faces a deadly challenge: decipher the mystery before each one is murdered.

In the Maya Gray series (which begins with Book #1—GIRL ONE: MURDER) FBI Special Agent Maya Gray, 39, has seen it all. She's one of BAU's rising stars and the go-to agent for hard-to-crack serial cases. When she receives a handwritten postcard promising to release 12 kidnapped women if she will solve 12 cold cases, she assumes it's a hoax.

Until the note mentions that, among the captives, is her missing sister.

Maya, shaken, is forced to take it seriously. The cases she's up against are some of the most difficult the FBI has ever seen. But the terms of his game are simple: If Maya solves a case, he will release one of the girls.

And if she fails, he will end a life.

In GIRL TWO: TAKEN (book #2), Maya must solve the murder of a female corrections officer. A seemingly black-and-white case, closed years ago, the local police refuse to take it up again. But as Maya delves into the world of prisons, correction officers and ex-cons, she quickly sees there is more there than meets the eye. She, it turns out, was not the only officer murdered. It was a serial. And this killer is more complex—and unpredictable—than anyone can imagine.

And if Maya doesn't solve this case soon, her own sister's life may be on the line.

Meanwhile, the first released "bunny" has given the FBI a promising lead on the killer's whereabouts—but are they walking into a trap?

In a race against time, and with her sister's life hanging in the balance, Maya must unravel the link between the 12 captives and end the killer's dark game once and for all. Is this killer toying with her? Does he truly have her sister? Will he ever give her back?

Or will Maya end up sucked too deep into this killer's twisted cat-and-mouse game to notice that she, herself, is the prey?

A complex psychological crime thriller full of twists and turns and packed with heart-pounding suspense, the MAYA GRAY mystery series will make you fall in love with a brilliant new female protagonist and keep you turning pages late into the night. It is a perfect addition for fans of Robert Dugoni, Rachel Caine, Melinda Leigh or Mary Burton.

Book #3 in the series—GIRL THREE TRAPPED—is now also available.

Molly Black

Debut author Molly Black is author of the MAYA GRAY MYSTERY series, comprising three books (and counting).

An avid reader and lifelong fan of the mystery and thriller genres, Molly loves to hear from you, so please feel free to visit www.mollyblackauthor.com to learn more and stay in touch.

BOOKS BY MOLLY BLACK

MAYA GRAY MYSTERY SERIES
GIRL ONE: MURDER (Book #1)
GIRL TWO: TAKEN (Book #2)
GIRL THREE: TRAPPED (Book #3)

Made in United States
Orlando, FL
12 May 2022

17820613R00114